FOOTHILL

BOOK 1: GENESIS AWAKENS

Akorede Adekoya &
Howard Haugom

To Fiona and the twins.
HH

TABLE OF CONTENTS

CHAPTER ONE

JERUSALEM 327 A.D.

Dust and dirt.

The air swirled with motes and particles of dust, filling every pathway and clinging to every surface.

Empress Helena waved her slender hand in a futile attempt to reduce the amount settling in the back of her throat. Her palanquin was covered with a thick layer, changing the white canvas to a dirty brown.

Empress Helena's personal guards stood beside her palanquin. The guards barely moved; their attention fixed ahead, searching the vicinity for any sign of trouble. They were dressed in full battle armor with their swords sheathed by their sides. In their right hands, they each held a lancea, a shorter and lighter version of a throwing spear. Soldiers watched over the laboring slaves as the slaves shoved molds of dirt into wheelbarrows while some stood by the entrance of a large cavern.

Helena tried to make herself comfortable. She had been on the road for weeks now to make sure she reached this site after she received word of the possibility of finding the Nazarene's cross. Her aged bones had felt every mile of the journey.

She could barely contain her anxiety as she watched slaves and laborers shovel dirt out of a large hole in the center of the room. Empress Helena felt a momentary pang of guilt. Her actions would be viewed by many as a desecration, but she was desperate.

She needed to find the nails.

Reports had come regarding a cavern located during the construction of a church over a pagan temple that had been pulled down. The church being built was dedicated to her son, Emperor Constantine the Great.

Some reports had coincided with the statement given by someone who had claimed to be a descendant of Joseph of Arimathea, the man who had taken Christ's body for burial in a tomb bought by Joseph. Joseph of Arimathea had intended the tomb to be his own resting place when the time came but had been moved to offer the tomb as Jesus's final resting place.

Maybe this would put an end to the dreams that plagued her sleep every night. Visions of war on a scale she could never imagine — machines of war that she couldn't understand.

Empress Helena had seen herself in that war. Herself, and yet, not herself: There had been a striking resemblance, but Helena could tell that it wasn't her. The look-alike looked different in the dream. She wore strange clothes and uttered incomprehensible words that she thought she could grasp if given time.

Her dreams also showed her a chamber beneath the earth that held power— a power that could alter the course of history, and she needed to find it.

The sound of commotion snapped Empress Helena back to the present. A man rushed to her palanquin and knelt before it.

"We have found it, your highness."

Empress Helena stood, her head touching the top of the palanquin, the quickening beat of her heart sending blood rushing to her head.

Could this be it?

She rushed in the direction the man had come from with her personal guards following. They created a way through the throng of slaves and laborers; the smell of sweat and earth from their bodies making Empress Helena wrinkle her nose.

Empress Helena entered the cavern and saw a large hole at the center.

She reached the edge of the pit the workers had dug and leaned over. Large pieces of wood littered the earth at the bottom of the hole. Helena looked for a way down and saw the top of a ladder sticking out of the pit. She turned to her guards to tell them to wait for her, but the guard in the lead moved ahead.

Calisto, the leader of her guards, jumped into the pit. Empress Helena watched as Calisto landed in the soft earth with his spear extended, the tip aimed at an imaginary adversary. Calisto quickly surveyed the pit, then snapped to attention.

Empress Helena sighed. She knew berating him for doing his job would only fall on deaf ears, for Calisto always blatantly ignored her directives when it came to her safety.

Helena took the wooden ladder made of tied sticks, as she didn't have the skill or recklessness to jump. She eyed Calisto, but he stared blankly ahead, feigning ignorance. Still, Helena could have sworn she saw the corner of his mouth lift in amusement.

Cheeky bastard!

The throng of power emanating from the pit as Helena reached the bottom drew Helena's attention away from Calisto. She bent down and felt the pieces of wood scattered around her feet.

Some were plain wood, thick, and broad across, but some made her fingers tingle.

The air vibrated with power.

Helena felt drawn to a corner of the pit where three large pieces of wood sat together. The air around these pieces shimmered, and Helena glanced at Calisto, who stood some meters behind her.

"You don't feel it?"

"Your highness?" Calisto's questioning gaze fell on Helena.

Helena turned back to the wood, her hand shaking as she reached out. Her fingers touched one of the pieces, and the world spun. Thunder boomed in the night, and the very earth under her feet seemed to shake and tremble.

Helena looked up to see that she was kneeling before a wooden cross.

A man hung on the cross with his head tilted forward. Helena felt drawn to the face of this man. The man's face was battered and bruised with blood caking the crown of thorns sitting on his head.

Dimly, she heard voices but couldn't make out what was said.

A Roman soldier walked to her side and looked up. The soldier held a spear in his hand, and Helena watched the soldier pierce the side of the man's body hanging on the cross.

"Your highness!"

The words shifted Empress Helena's focus back to the present, and she saw Calisto's face looking down at her in worry. Helena turned to see that she was lying on the ground beside the wood she had touched.

What had just happened?

Was this real?

Empress Helena tried to orientate herself. She could feel the damp earth beneath her palms and realized she was in the pit.

She remembered the night air caressing her cheeks while the sound of boots approached her, crunching fine sand as the Roman soldier had stood beside her.

Helena took Calisto's offered hand and got to her knees. She swept aside the earth around the wood. As magical as the wood had been, a more potent power drew her.

Her fingers touched something warm and solid, and Helena gasped, but no vision came this time.

3

She parted the soil around the piece of nail that held more value than anything else. It was heptagonal and about nine inches in length. Helena reverently picked up the powerful nail.

This was it.

The tingling she had felt had become a buzz, the air around the nail distorted and warped as power radiated from it.

It was one of the three nails that had pierced the hands and feet of Jesus the Christ — the one called the Nazarene.

She saw another nail close to the first.

One more.

She dug with her fingers, frantic and anxious.

A scream pierced the silence that had engulfed the room. Someone had screamed in pain, and Calisto rose to his feet.

"Your highness, we must make haste and leave this place now."

"Not yet."

"I must insist, your highness. People have entered the room above us."

Calisto moved to pull Helena to her feet, but she jerked his hand away.

"Don't you see, Calisto? We must find it. The third nail."

Helena turned her attention back to searching for the last nail. The clang of metal against metal filled the air as a battle erupted above them.

A scream was cut short, and a body toppled into the pit.

Calisto rushed to the body and looked down.

A slave gurgled and spat out blood as he choked, a wide gash across his throat, bleeding his life essence out.

Calisto turned to see Empress Helena get up, her eyes gleaming with a strange light and a fanatical grin on her face.

"We have it." She waved what looked like three large nails at Calisto, but his attention was already on the commotion topside.

Calisto waited for Helena to get to his side before they approached the wooden ladder.

"Wait here, your highness." Calisto dropped his spear and drew his short sword. He nodded once to Helena and climbed the ladder.

Calisto got to the top and looked around in confusion. The slaves and laborers were huddled in a corner of the room in fear as they watched the battle. His fellow guards seemed to be battling a...*single soldier*? That could not be possible.

4

Calisto stared in amazement.

The empress's guards were the last of the disbanded Praetorian guards — soldiers trained from childhood to fight. They were the best of the best, handpicked by him, and they were all dying swiftly.

Calisto watched the lone assailant duck under a swinging arm as one of the guards tried to take his head. The assailant moved quickly.

The assailant's sword pierced the guard in the armpit, the blade ripping his muscles and bursting out of his collarbone. The soldier dropped to the ground, twitched for a moment, and then went still.

The remaining two guards backed away in fear as the assailant advanced towards the pit.

Calisto walked to the assassin slowly, watching the way the man held his sword. A calm came over Calisto as he released a breath and focused on the man attacking his men. The assailant wore a white toga and plain sandals. Bloodstains gave the assailant a menacing air as he walked towards the pit.

As Calisto passed the two guards backing away, he commanded, "Protect the empress."

He stopped outside the assassin's striking distance.

"You have attacked the property of Empress Helena, mother of Emperor Constantine the Great. Your violent actions will bring death to you today."

The assassin stopped by the pit and looked at Calisto. He raised his bloodstained sword and pointed it at Empress Helena.

"The woman has something that belongs to me by right. I have wandered the earth for centuries looking for it and have now found it in her custody. I am here to collect what is mine."

Calisto bent his knees and arms, his short sword held diagonally across his body.

"Your journey ends here."

The assassin smiled and lifted his sword, taking the same pose as Calisto. For a fraction of a second, Calisto registered that the assassin was trained like the Praetorian guards, and he noticed how the man's sword curved towards his neck.

Helena watched as Calisto climbed the ladder, and a moment later, two guards stared down at her.

"What is going on?" she demanded.

"An assassin, your highness," one of the guards replied.

The guards looked hesitant and confused. One glanced behind him, and Helena heard the clanging of metal clashing against metal.

If there was an assassin, being in the pit was the worst possible position. Helena climbed the ladder and gasped as she reached the top.

Bodies of her guards and slaves were scattered across the room. Other slaves, who had survived, were trying to make themselves invisible, shrinking into a corner.

Helena looked around and saw Calisto fighting the assassin, and her heart almost failed her. She had seen enough gladiator fights to know that Calisto was on the defensive. The assailant moved with uncanny speed, able to read Calisto's moves before Calisto made them.

Calisto was losing.

Calisto saw the blade coming for his neck and ducked under the swing. He lunged with his sword, aiming for the assassin's armpit as the man had done to one of the guards.

The assassin struck Calisto's sword to the side, and Calisto almost lost his grip on his sword.

The blow rang up his arm, and it went numb for a second.

The assassin retaliated with a lunge of his own, and Calisto leaped to the side. His numb arm couldn't react quickly enough, and Calisto felt pain burn through his arm as the assassin's blade cut.

He ignored the pain to stay focused and twisted his arm slightly, turning his attack into a short swing, aiming for the assassin's throat.

The assassin predicted the move and tried to back away, but the tip of his sword sliced the assassin's throat, and Calisto smiled.

The assassin staggered backward.

"It's been decades since someone cut my skin," the assassin said, his voice strained.

Calisto's smile faded as the wound sewed itself back up, and the assassin's neck was whole again.

"What are you?" Calisto whispered.

"I am Lucilius. Cursed and destined to wander the earth, never dying. My belief is that the nails that woman holds will change that."

"You are an abomination."

Lucilius doesn't reply and attacks again.

❖

Helena watched as Calisto and the assassin exchanged a flurry of blows. She puts her hand to her mouth as the assassin's sword swung close to Calisto's face. Calisto would immediately parry and strike back, but the assassin seemed faster.

Calisto grunted as the assassin's blade sliced through his thigh. He tried to raise his sword to block the incoming thrust, but he was a moment slower, fatigue settling in his muscles.

Calisto moved his body aside at the last minute, but the assassin's sword pierced his side.

"It is over, soldier. You fought with honor."

Calisto watched as the assassin rose his arm to swing his blade. Calisto could barely move his arm, and he tried to catch his breath.

"Protect the em —"

Calisto's eyes widened in surprise as Empress Helena rushed towards the assassin.

Lucilius sensed the attack and pulled out a dagger from his side as Helena reached him. Calisto knew Helena wouldn't be able to stop her momentum and would impale herself on the end of the assassin's dagger. He gritted his teeth and rushed forward, splitting the assassin's attention between him and Empress Helena.

Grabbing the assassin's hand that held the dagger, Calisto pulled the assassin's hand towards himself and grunted in pain as the assassin's sword pierced his stomach.

It was a killing move, and Calisto knew the end had come, but he refused to let go of the arm that held the dagger.

The assassin looked on as Helena swung her arm across his face. He screamed in pain as the nail in Helena's hand bit into his face.

Lucilius staggered back, and Helena dropped to her knees beside Calisto.

"Run, your highness... ordinary weapons can't hurt him."

Helena ignored Calisto's plea and grabbed him under the arms. She staggered under the added weight as she tried to lift Calisto to his feet.

"Can you get up?"

"No, your highness. This is the end for me." Helena looked down and saw Calisto trying his best to stem the blood gushing from the wound to his stomach. Helena bit her lip in despair. She turned to see the assassin hold his head and scream.

Had he gone mad?

7

Helena heard the sound of sandals slapping on the earth and turned to the entrance.

An elderly man dressed in a long white robe entered the chambers. He had white hair that fell below his shoulders and a leathery, weather-beaten face. He walked with a vitality and strength that was in contrast to his appearance and stood before her.

"I see you have found it, Empress Helena."

The man looked vaguely familiar, like a distant relative who you met as a child. The elderly man exuded trust, but Helena fought the notion.

"Who are you?" she asked cautiously.

Calisto groaned, and Helena's attention returned to him. She could see that he was dying. Tears trailed down her cheeks, and she heard Calisto's breathing become shallower. He had saved her life. She didn't know why she had rushed at the assassin. Maybe Calisto wouldn't have been hurt if she had remained in the pit. What had come over her?

She would never have been able to strike the assassin if Calisto hadn't given his life away by holding the assassin's hand.

"We have to be away from here. He comes," the elderly man said.

Helena glanced at the assassin, who was still screaming in pain in a corner of the cavern.

"Who comes? I'm not leaving Calisto to die here."

"Then you would kill us all. Can you not feel it yet? His slaves will soon be here, and they will take those away from you." The elderly man nodded towards the nails clutched in Helena's hands.

She frowned.

How did the man know the value of what she carried?

She had thought the whispers had been from the slaves gathered in the corner, but when she listened intently, the voices grew louder and weren't coming from the slaves.

The nails bring power.

He who has the nails becomes the emperor.

Destroy the empire. Rule the kingdom.

Helena shook her head in a bid to silence the whispers.

The elderly man bent over Calisto and whispered something into his ear.

"We have to go, now." The elderly man stretched out his hand towards Helena.

"I will not leave him."

"You can only die if you remain here. He has done his part, and I promise you will see him again."

"Go, my highness." Calisto struggled to his feet and slumped back in exhaustion. "Go and live."

Soldiers rushed into the chamber as the elderly man grabbed Helena's arm and pulled her to him. She felt the aura of power around him.

"Who are you?" she asked again.

The elderly man looked into Helena's eyes. "You may know me as Merlin."

He waved his hand, and in a flash, the world went silent and a brilliant white.

CHAPTER TWO

Gen felt a bump and slowly opened her eyes.

She stifled a yawn and looked at the passenger seated beside her. The middle-aged Asian woman had her head tilted back and was snoring gently.

Gen tried to ignore the woman and looked out the window of the plane. Endless clouds filled her sight, and she wondered what it would be like to be free and not have a care in the world.

To just soar and let everything…go.

Ladies and gentlemen, we have just been cleared to land at John G. Diefenbaker International airport. Please make sure that your seat belt is securely fastened. The flight attendants are currently…

Gen mentally tuned out the flight attendant's announcement and leaned back. She was going home, and it was bittersweet. Gen had a lot of fun memories of growing up. Her granddad had stayed with her parents at the ranch…or *had it been the other way round?*

Growing up had been a wonderful experience, but it also brought the bitter feeling tugging within.

She had been closer to her granddad than her parents, and he was the reason she was going back home because her granddad had passed away.

She tried not to grip the armrest too hard as the plane made its final descent.

❖

Gen moved out of the way of a couple running into each other's arms and looked around. The airport was busy with people rushing to their various terminals. She saw the Asian woman walking away and waved at her. The woman was visiting her grandchildren for the first time.

10

Announcements from the PA speakers ran every few seconds, announcing arrivals or expected times of arrivals.

Gen took a deep breath. The very air seemed to sparkle with vitality. Crisp and clean.

"Genesis! Genesis!"

Gen cringed.

Only one person called her by her full name. Gen turned to the source of the voice calling her name and smiled. Her mum stood by a shop and waved, and Gen walked over.

Her mother was in her late forties but looked younger with slightly greying hair that stopped at the nape of her neck. Her beautifully curved eyebrows sat over sweeping eyelids. She held herself with an air of dignity that was both warm and inviting. She had on an elegant navy-blue blouse with matching shoes and purse — a picture of poise and beauty. Something Gen knew she failed at.

Her father stood beside her mum. A gawky man in his early fifties with spectacles slightly skewed or, as Gen liked to say, 'having a nap.'

Gen's father looked like he had hurriedly put on his brown pants and creased checkered shirt underneath a dark-brown jacket. His hair was uncombed, and he had on loafers that didn't match the color of his jacket.

Just how she remembered and loved them.

Gen gave her parents a deep hug and tried to smile as they looked her up and down.

"You've lost so much weight, honey. What have you been doing to yourself?"

"Let her be, dear. She just got here," her father defended her.

"Mum!"

This was stability. This Gen understood.

"I was in school, Mum. You know, trying to get my degree in business management."

"That's not an excuse, dear. Your dad and I passed through the same college, and in my time, I was the reigning—"

"She knows, dear."

Gen's father picked up her carry-on bag, and they headed for the exit.

"But does she know? That's the question." Gen's mother put on a stern expression, but Gen smiled and shook her head.

"Love you too, Mum."

Her dad gave her an encouraging smile.

"Let's get you home."

Gen could only agree.

❖

Dundurn was a small town.

Gen felt the warm breeze blow her hair as they drove through town. She nodded as people waved at them. Everybody literally knew everybody.

When a town has a population that runs into only hundreds, anonymity was a far-fetched dream.

She saw a couple of faces that were strange to her, but the town seemed the same. The vet clinic was still by the corner of Mrs. Mayfield's bakery shop. The barbershop still seemed empty, and the *Dundurn Gazette* building still looked dilapidated and about to crumble.

Maybe this was what she needed, Gen thought.

She craved stability right now. She didn't want to scare her parents, but Gen had recently felt lost and overwhelmed, hating life at university in Toronto and struggling with her course, but Gen wanted to please her mother. Every Isherwood woman attended the University of Toronto. Gen couldn't be the exception.

The town had one major road entering and leaving the city, and they quickly left the city behind as they drove to the family ranch. Gen watched the landscape rushing by as her father drove their black SUV through the gate and into the farm. Gen noted the metal arch over the gateway as they passed. The name of the ranch was boldly etched on the metal.

The 'Triple 7 Ranch.'

Gen looked around as they drove to the house.

Nothing about the ranch seemed to have changed.

She could see the barn some feet from the house. The farmland was behind the house, but Gen caught a glimpse of wheat arranged in neat lines.

Everything seemed the same.

Gen waited for the bark of Whisky, their German shepherd. Whisky always came out of wherever she was when she heard the van coming into the ranch.

"Where's Whisky?" she asked after a couple of seconds.

"Oh, Whisky passed on last year, honey," her mum said.

"No! What happened?" Gen turned to her mum, who was in the back seat.

"Some hooligans out from Saskatoon ran her over, honey," her mother explained.

12

"Sheriff Liam says we have to be extra careful now that some new businesses have settled at Saskatoon."

"Who would do such a thing to Whisky?"

It seemed some things changed after all.

❖

Gen turned the knob of the bedroom door, and it creaked as it swung open. She stood in the doorway and peered into the bedroom. Memories flooded her senses, and Gen traveled to a time when the world made sense.

She heard giggling and the patter of running feet as she remembered a time when all that mattered was finding the best places to hide when she played with her grandfather. She had been an only child but had never felt the loneliness others in her position felt.

Her grandfather had been her friend, confidante, parent, and guardian. He had been more a parent than her mum and dad.

Not that she had anything against her parents; she loved them, and they were just that — her parents.

But her granddad had been the one she ran to when she needed help with her homework.

Her grandfather had been the one to read her stories and tuck her in at night after making sure there weren't any scary monsters underneath her bed.

Gen stepped into the bedroom.

Silence filled the bedroom, but a silence that told a whole lot.

Gen squatted and almost smiled as she remembered sitting down with granddad for her afternoon tea, her little dolls making a semi-circle around her, with her grandad just outside it. Her granddad would sit there with a smile and a twinkle in his eyes.

So many memories.

The bed was freshly made. Gen walked over to it and sat down. She looked around and noticed that some of her clothes were still in the opened closet.

The hinges didn't seem to have been fixed after all this time.

She had been at peace in this house. Her grandfather's presence was a comfort that had protected her from the world.

She remembered his stories.

Stories that she found out much later were from the Bible. She had been fascinated with his stories.

Moses and the Red Sea.

He always said to understand how Moses had believed in God despite the circumstances facing Moses — Pharaoh, with his large army of over two hundred thousand foot soldiers and more than fifty thousand horse riders charging towards Moses, who was stuck with the Red Sea behind him. Moses raised his staff and parted the Red Sea.

Gen would gasp at that.

It had almost been as if she could hear the roaring of the waves as they parted and see the dry land appearing for Moses and the children of Israel to cross.

Then, there was David and Goliath. This story had been Gen's favorite. She loved a good underdog story, and her grandfather had known how to tell it right.

Gen couldn't tell if it had been her imagination, but she could have sworn that she had heard the clanging sound of swords on shields as they beat in rhythm to the drums of war.

David had been a kid and had done the unbelievable. He had killed Goliath, the giant — the giant the whole army of Israel had feared.

David and Goliath's story had made Gen more daring, believing that she could also do the impossible.

After hearing the story, she had walked around with a wooden sword — more a broken branch than a sword — but she had felt brave. And confident. And bold.

Oh, how her grandfather loved to tell such beautiful stories! Stories of virtues that Gen had tried to live by but had failed miserably.

She remembered him sitting by her bed; his face wrinkled with age.

It was a kind face. Her granddad seemed always to have a kind word for everyone.

Gen didn't think she had ever seen her granddad angry.

She missed him greatly.

Gen felt hot tears course down her cheeks.

CHAPTER THREE

Dinner was a quiet affair.

There was a silence that no one seemed eager to break.

They sat around the small dining table in the kitchen. The kitchen was spacious, with a cupboard by a window.

Gen twirled her fork around her plate of food.

"You have to eat something, honey," said her mum.

Gen continued turning her fork.

"How did granddad die?"

"I told you, honey, he slumped and just...passed on."

"Granddad was never sick. He was probably the healthiest person in this house."

"He was old, Genny," her dad said.

"But it doesn't make sense. Did granddad have a heart attack? Had he had one before?"

Gen dropped her fork on her plate, abandoning her half-eaten spaghetti and meatballs.

"Honey, the coroner said his heart failed. Old age does that, you know."

Gen tried to picture her grandfather keeling over, but all she could see was his vibrant smile and cheerful disposition.

Was she to blame?

Was it because she hadn't kept in touch?

Could he have missed her that much?

"Genny?"

"Huh?"

Gen looked up to see her parents staring at her. She saw a flash of worry on her mum's face, but it was gone as quickly as it had appeared.

"Sorry, what did you say?"

"I asked if Theo has called you. He does know you are back, right?" Her mum had an expectant look that Gen chose to ignore.

"No, Mum. Theo and I haven't been keeping in touch."

"I'm sure he knows you're back, being the sheriff's son. Do you know that he's the deputy sheriff now? Got sworn in last spring, right, dear?" Gen's dad nodded as he ate his meal.

"Good for him," Gen stated.

"You two used to be like two peas in a pod. Always together."

"We were kids, Mum."

"I know, but that's how fruitful relationships blossom, honey."

Gen tried to concentrate on her food.

"Theo is such a nice young man. I told him he could check on you anytime. Hope you don't mind, honey."

Gen tried not to glare at her mum. She turned to her dad instead, who suddenly found a string of pasta extremely fascinating.

Gen welcomed the silence that followed with open arms.

Gen stared at herself in the bathroom mirror. A young woman in her early twenties stared back with bags under her eyes that make-up couldn't hide.

Gen raised her hand. There was a slight tremor in it that she had been able to hide from her parents throughout dinner, but the craving was getting unbearable. Gen placed her hand back on the sink.

Her time in university had been rough. She had barely been able to keep an average GPA, and her lecturers had begun to pressure her to keep up.

That's when she'd heard of 'molly' — a stimulant to take the edge off. The drug reduced anxiety attacks, but what the dealer didn't advertise was how addictive the drug was.

Gen had stopped using when she'd heard of her grandfather's death, but the drug wasn't entirely out of her system.

Gen walked to her bed and lay down. She had sworn she would honor her grandfather's memory by not taking any more molly, but the yearning to open her suitcase was intense.

Gen closed her eyes, trying to ignore the whispers around her.

Only a pill. Just to take the edge off.
Your grandfather wouldn't want to see you so sad.
You know that's why you brought the bottle. You need molly.

Gen covered her ears with the pillow.

You need molly.

The words were almost a chant, and Gen tried to block them out. It was going to be a long night.

❖

Gen woke, feeling terrible. She had barely slept.

Her night had been filled with dreams of a shadow chasing her. There was darkness she couldn't see but had been sure was real — at least, as real as any dream could be.

The darkness had brought decay and a sense of corruption. A lingering smell of rotten eggs had filled her room.

Gen entered the kitchen to see her mum preparing breakfast.

"Up for some pancakes, honey?"

"I'll pass, Mum."

Gen dragged a chair and sat down.

Her mum poured her a cup of coffee, which she gladly accepted.

"You don't look too good."

"Couldn't sleep."

"You know, there's an article about how lack of eating can cause insomnia."

"I'm good, Mum. Just have a lot on my mind."

"What could be troubling you?"

"Oh, I don't know, maybe the fact that I just lost my granddad."

Gen sighed as she saw her mum drop the coffee pot and head to the frying pan on the stove.

"Sorry, mum. I just don't get it. Granddad's your father, and you and dad don't seem upset that he's gone."

Gen's mum walked back to the table and took a seat facing Gen.

"Your granddad...well, let's just say that he's always seemed larger than life. It was inevitable that he would die, honey. He was over seventy years old, and we all die eventually."

"I know, Mum. It's just that you don't seem sad about it."

Gen watched her mum bite her lower lip and frowned. Her mum only did that when she was uncertain or unable to make a decision.

"Why would you say that? How would you know what I'm feeling?"

"I don't know. I...just know."

"That doesn't make any sense, honey. You can't 'not know' and just know at the same time."

"I just have this feeling that you and dad know something that I don't. Was granddad in pain?"

"Look, honey, it's not your fault that granddad died, okay? People die. He was old, and it was his time."

Gen watched as her mum went to check the pancakes.

"The memorial service is in two days' time," her mum said.

"We'll be using the barn for the service. Remind me to call Mrs. Alice and Emma. We'll need to clear out some of granddad's things to the shed to create enough space."

"I can do that!" Gen quickly said.

"No, it's too much work for you."

"I can start, and you guys join in later."

"Are you sure, honey?"

Gen nodded. She needed the distraction.

Gen walked into the barn and looked around. The ranch had once flourished a long time ago, but Gen's granddad had seemed content to allow the farm to become a home over the years.

The barn seemed as she remembered it.

Gen walked around, the smell of hay and wood filling her nostrils. There was a stable at the side, but now it housed only a couple of horses, Ginger and Gale. They had been draft horses, but time had eroded their strength, and they were part of the 'Triple 7' family.

On the other side of the barn was granddad's workspace. Gen sorted through the equipment on the workbench.

Her grandfather had called it his mini-smithy. She would always find him here hammering a horseshoe or molding a farm implement.

Gen ran her fingers over the tools.

She remembered her grandfather telling her that everyone was like a farm tool, molded for a particular use.

She had been eight then and hadn't understood what her granddad had meant.

So, what had she been molded for? she wondered. *Was her life an endless pattern of hurt?*

The urge to go to her room and take molly was still strong.

Gen saw a bound leather book and frowned. Her granddad always kept his Bible by his bedside table, so it was strange finding it here in his workspace.

She picked up her grandfather's Bible gently and slowly flipped through the pages. She could see that he had underlined a lot of verses, sometimes entire chapters. Gen read through some of them. A favorite saying of her grandfather came to mind — the person who trusted God will not only do what Christ did but even more remarkable things.

Gen flicked to the end of the Bible and saw a piece of folded paper tucked in the last page. Her hand shook as she saw her name on the note. She immediately recognized her granddad's handwriting, and with shaking fingers, Gen unfolded the note and read:

My warrior princess,

I know that my leaving is hard for you, but you are strong. Always keep that in mind, and don't forget all that I have taught you. Remember, God is always there to help you and guide you. All you have to do is trust Him. And just like Moses, move straight forward, even when the road ahead seems insurmountable.

Remember what you do when you need to focus. Find yourself again, for you are not alone.

Gen wiped the tears from her eyes and reread the note.

Had he known what she was going through? The letter seemed too direct, almost as if he had been with her through her ordeals.

And what did he mean by the last line?

Remember what you do when you need to focus.

And the part about finding herself again, for she wasn't alone.

Had he left his Bible here for her to find?

It seemed impossible, and Gen flipped through the pages again but found nothing.

Remember what you do when you need to focus.

There was only one thing she did when she needed to make a decision.

Gen looked around the workspace.

She remembered that she had always wanted to be like her grandfather and had taken to working the forge as he did.

Gen found what she was looking for.

She hadn't been good at making anything decent, but that hadn't been the purpose of striking the hammer to the mold. The rhythmic hammering had been soothing to her, allowing her to think and plan. That's what her grandfather had meant.

The anvil and stump weren't too large, so she could drag it out of the corner where it had been placed. Gen picked up a hammer and braced herself. She wasn't planning on forging anything. She just wanted to clear her mind.

Gen lifted the hammer and brought it down hard on the anvil. As the hammer struck the anvil, the vibration raced up her arm and up to her shoulders.

Gen smiled. It had been so long since she had done this, but it gave her a wonderful feeling. It was like coming home.

Gen struck the anvil repeatedly, building a steady momentum. Her lack of practice showed as she was panting after a few seconds of pounding on the anvil, but Gen didn't relent.

Her granddad's words flooded her soul.

You are made in the image of your Creator.
You are a chosen generation, a royal priesthood.
Greater is He that is in you than he that is in the world.
Don't be afraid of when the wicked are destroyed, for God is your
confidence and shall strengthen you continually.

Her granddad's words made hope well up again in Gen's heart, and as she struck the anvil repeatedly, she felt something she hadn't in a long time.

Joy filled her heart.

The motel room looked cheap, with a worn-out spring mattress and threadbare bedsheet, but Mark didn't mind. Mark stood, staring out of the window. His view was a parking lot, all concrete and cars. He took a minute to observe the area and then saw a car come into the lot and slow down. A middle-aged man and a much younger woman climbed out. An elderly woman ambled across the parking lot, heading towards the reception. Mark turned away from the window and walked to the minibar, fetching a can of beer.

While it wasn't to his taste, it was the only thing stocked in the bar.

Mark walked to the springy bed and sat down. A manila envelope was on the bed, and he picked it up.

The instructions had been specific.

To the day.

The client had been adamant. Not a day earlier and not a day later. He was to come to Saskatoon the day before and open the envelope the day after.

Mark had frowned over the client's request but hadn't asked any questions.

The pay, after all, was worth the eccentricity.

Mark looked at his sports wristwatch.

10:00 a.m.

He tore open the manila envelope and poured its contents onto the bed.

A portrait of a beautiful woman in her early twenties slid out of the envelope. The woman had her face away from the photographer and only her side profile was captured. The picture still captured the woman's flaming red hair tied with a ribbon to keep it away from her face.

Mark frowned.

He had been explicit to the client.

His company was in the protection business. This cloak and dagger routine pointed to a hit.

Mark pushed the portrait aside and saw a micro flash drive.

He still had the choice of rejecting the job. That was always a clause in every contract he took. He would check what the drive contained and then know what his next step would be.

N

CHAPTER FOUR

The elderly man hadn't lived this long by making careless mistakes, so he took his time as he studied the building's layout.

The man looked to be in his mid-fifties, with greying hair and a wrinkled face caused by smiling too much. He didn't mind the wrinkles. He felt they gave him character and didn't scare the little children away. And he didn't mind smiling.

There hadn't been much to smile about for a very long time, and then, his family had grown up. He had watched them become people he could be proud of, and bringing them up had brought lots of smiles to his face.

The whirling of a security camera brought the man back to the present. Everything he did, he did for his family. He had to make sure his family remained safe, especially with the vision he had recently seen.

The man hid in the shrubs facing a building he had been watching. Scaling the gate had been easy, and he had spotted the security camera mounted on the gate pillar. The tricky part would be getting into the building without being seen. He needed to get into the building to confirm a suspicion, and if his suspicions were correct, he might need to collect his family and run. That would be a shame. He had grown to like the place and the people. But he wasn't a stranger to leaving everything behind and moving on. He had done it countless times.

The man watched the camera's rotation, seeing the pattern and the time intervals it took to sweep over his hiding place. He waited for the camera to move away from his position before running to the door of the building.

This was the tricky part.

There was a keypad by the side of the door, and the man punched in a series of numbers. He grinned when the door clicked open. As weird as it would seem if he told anybody, he had seen the combination in a dream. He would probably be laughed at, but he had learned to trust such insights over time.

He had the uncanny talent of seeing glimpses of the future. He could see moments before they happened, or sometimes see years ahead. Sometimes, what he saw was as clear as day, while other times, it was riddled with obscurity. This had been one such time when the sight (as he had come to term it) was crystal clear.

He needed to check this building, and the combination of the electronic door had come to him. The man allowed the door to swing open slowly. He had staked out the place for a couple of days and hadn't seen anyone, but that didn't mean there couldn't be surprises waiting for him.

The door opened to a foyer with doors leading to rooms. The gloomy feel of the hallway didn't bother the man. There were worse things than the dark, and he had tangled with some of them.

The man focused and tried to sense the object he had come for. His senses expanded, and he could feel the energy emanating from different things in the house. A strong pulsing power radiated from the room facing him.

The man crept to the door and felt the wood. He was in the right place. A sense of excitement crept into his heart.

This could tip the scale in the war he was fighting. What lay behind the door was an object of power, and in the wrong hands, it could be devastating. The man's senses swept forward, feeling the resonance in the thing in the room. He twisted the knob slowly and walked into the room.

A single high stool stood in the middle of the room with a nail on a velvet pillow. The man frowned and looked around. Something was off. The object on the high stool was an anomaly with the house itself, and it could only mean one thing — the place was a trap.

The man extended his senses around and detected the traps set in the room. There was a containment spell that had triggered when he entered the room. The spell trapped anything within its sphere, but the man wasn't bothered by the containment spell. It wasn't made to hold beings like him. Other spells were erected to protect the nail on the high stool, but the man quickly disabled them.

The man walked to the high stool and picked up the nail. His smile quickly turned to a frown as his gaze fell on it.

It was a fake.

The room exploded with fire as another spell triggered. In a heartbeat, the man moved. He stretched out his hand to the raging fire around him, and a gust of mighty wind rushed from the center of his hand. The wind swirled and twisted a few inches above his hand. Within seconds, it became a whirlwind, sucking the raging fire around him. The fire disappeared into the vortex created by the wind, and the man looked around.

23

The trap showed the thinking of only one man.

"Come out now, Atticus." The elderly man waited and turned when the door opened.

A man in a police uniform walked into the room and clapped as he stood near the door.

"Where is Atticus?" the elderly man demanded.

"How do you know it isn't him standing before you?" The man in the police uniform remained by the door with a smile plastered on his face.

"You may change your face, Remus, but you can't change who or what you are," the elderly man said.

Remus clutched his heart in a mocking gesture of being wounded by the elderly man's words.

"You wound me. Atticus couldn't be here, but he left a gift for you."

The elderly man raised an eyebrow at Remus and folded his arms while tapping his lip.

"I can see that he still has poor taste."

"Well, who am I to judge? I told Atticus the spell wouldn't even scratch you, but Atticus believed the simplicity of the trap would be what surprised you."

"Oh, I'm surprised, all right. If Atticus created a powerful spell, I would have sensed it immediately. He was hoping the fire would surprise me and harm me before I could counter. What I don't understand is why he left you behind." The elderly man frowned.

Atticus wouldn't leave the fate of his creation to a simpleton like Remus.

Which meant only one thing — Atticus was still around.

The elderly man spun his hand in a small circle and muttered a spell under his breath. The elderly man's eyes glowed, and Remus took a step back. The elderly man surveyed the room quickly. He had activated an ability that allowed him to see the life force of living things.

Remus churned with a boiling mist of darkness some meters before him, and the man looked around and noticed they were alone.

The elderly man frowned.

Remus was robust in his ability to shapeshift and disguise his appearance, but against someone stronger than him, Remus was a coward.

Something was wrong.

Remus smiled at the elderly man and waved.

A second explosion triggered, and the elderly man saw a raging inferno gather at the center of the room. The fire took the shape of a beast and bellowed.

Swiftly, before the elderly man could react, the fire enveloped every-thing in the containment area. The elderly man felt heat scorch his skin as the fire surrounded him. This was the real trap. The first fire had been a distraction.

Remus had stepped out of the containment area moments before the fire had erupted. The elderly man watched as Remus stared at him for a moment and then walked away.

It was a well-executed trap, the elderly man conceded, but they had forgotten one thing — he was a legend.

The heat slapped his face but stopped an inch from his body.

He had learned long ago to cast a barrier spell over his body. It had taken him years, but now it came by reflex. He rarely entered a dangerous situation without his barrier.

The elderly man muttered under his breath and clapped his hands together.

There was a roar, and everything within the containment area ceased to exist. The fire vanished, and the elderly man walked to the door. The elderly man stopped and looked down, spotting the fake nail. The nail had fallen off the stool during the attack and was on the ground. He picked up the nail and studied it.

This was what had brought him here. The nail exuded power, and it had been that power that he had sensed. The man rubbed his thumb against the nail and grimaced when some tiny particles fell off. He continued rubbing the nail until he removed all the iron coating and saw that the nail was just an ordinary one.

This was unexpected. His suspicions were confirmed, though.

His family was in danger, for the accursed were here.

The man walked out of the room and out of the building.

Gen was dreaming.

A feeling of terror washed over her as she ran. She stumbled through the forest, knowing she had to get out of there before the creature chasing her caught up with her.

Something horrible raced after her, and she could hear the mocking laughter as the thing pursued.

I see you.

Gen opened her mouth to scream, but just like in her other recent dreams, an endless silence issued from her lips. The laughter behind her came closer, and Gen knew she couldn't allow the darkness to meet up with her.

The path before her was crooked and rough. She stumbled and scrambled to her feet. She could sense the direction she needed to go and headed that way.

She had to get to the barn. There was safety there. She didn't know how she knew, but she didn't question that feeling.

Gen looked over her shoulder and saw the darkness that was chasing her inch closer. A tendril of black smoke shot towards her. Gen tried to dodge but felt pain as the thin thread of black pierced her calf.

The laughter was everywhere. It surrounded Gen, feeling her soul and trying to taint it.

You will fail, child. Submit to me and let it go.
Never!

Gen's wordless protest gave her power, and she bolted out of the woods. The scenery before her changed, and she realized she was on her granddad's ranch.

Gen sobbed as she dashed for the barn. She felt the darkness beating at her back as she ran towards it.

Submit, child. You are alone. You will die alone.

The barn loomed large. Gen stretched out a hand but felt a rope wrap around her ankle and pull, slamming her to the ground. She grunted in pain and felt a burning sensation as a tendril wrapped around her ankle.

You are worthless, nail bearer. You have failed.

Gen saw the barn recede as she was dragged backward. She dug her hands into the earth, breaking her fingernails as she tried to find purchase. She couldn't fail now.

Gen remembered her granddad's words and summoned courage. A part of her knew she had to respond to the fear building in her heart.

She wasn't alone. She had her parents. She had her granddad's teachings and words inside of her, and those words were life for her.

I am not alone, Gen screamed into the darkness. I am never alone, for greater is He in me than any situation in the world, including you.

The tendril around her ankle shivered. Words rushed into her mind, and she uttered them into the swelling darkness. Gen felt a warmth gather inside her, and it quickly spread. The tendril recoiled in pain as the feeling reached her feet. She had stopped some meters from the barn, and Gen got to her feet. Darkness so immense loomed before her.

You have failed.
There is nothing left for you here. Your grandfather is dead.
He suffered greatly before he died.
You left him alone. He hated you before he died, cursing your name. You are worthless.

Gen knew the lie for what it was. Her granddad never hated anyone. His note for her had been one of love, and she had felt it in her heart. This thing was a deceiver.

Gen stared firmly into the darkness.

You have lost. You seek to sow hate and discord in my heart, but you have failed.

Gen remembered the darkness had withdrawn when she had spoken her granddad's words — words from the Bible. Words that now filled her heart, for she had a better understanding of them now.

God loved her. Regardless of what she had done or what her past had been. God's love was unconditional.

God was also with her, sharing her burdens and lifting her sorrows. That was why her granddad always had a smile on his face. She was never alone.

She remembered somewhere in the Bible words that were appropriate for this moment.

Get behind me, deceiver. I am a child of the Highest.

The darkness raged and stormed, but Gen ignored it and walked back to the barn.

Gen groaned and opened her eyes.

The dream had felt so real. She winced as she looked down at her ankle and saw a thin line across it.

Had she really been asleep?

Gen fell back on the bed as she tried to remember her dream. Waking had eroded the memory and had left her with imperfect images and recollection.

She had been running from something, but she wasn't sure what it was. An evil that had tried to consume her. She also vaguely remembered winning by the words she had said. She had spoken words that had come from the teachings she had as a child.

Gen closed her eyes and tried to sleep again.

She didn't notice a shadow like that of a man walk out of the bedroom, leaving behind a lingering feeling of power woven in the room to keep her safe.

CHAPTER FIVE

The barn had been cleaned up for the memorial service. A wooden stand with a picture of Gen's grandfather stood at the front of the aisle.

There was no coffin, since the body had been cremated, according to his wishes.

Gen sat in the front seat with her mum and dad beside her and glanced around in surprise. It looked like the whole town had come to say goodbye to her granddad.

Granddad had been a member of the only parish in Dundurn, and Gen remembered that he and the minister had been close. The minister had come with a vocalist, who had sung an inspiring requiem.

The minister cleared his throat to get everybody's attention.

"Mr. Gourdeau doesn't need an introduction. He was a gentle soul who had a passion for God and for humanity. That's why we'll be taking our scripture from the book of Mark, chapter 12, verses 30 and 31. Here, Jesus admonishes us to love God with all our heart, soul, and mind, and to love our neighbor as ourselves."

The minister looked at the people gathered in the barn.

"Melvin Gourdeau was a man who loved God completely, and he loved the people of Dundurn. He went out of his way to make sure anyone that met him left better than when he came. He gave his all for this community, and we are sad to have lost someone like him."

Gen held back tears. Her mum dabbed at her wet eyes with a hankie as her dad held her mum's hand in comfort.

She had drifted away from her family the last two years. Even though the university hadn't been far away, she had found a reason to remain on campus or had followed her friends to Vancouver.

And there had been molly. She had become dependent on the drug and knew which parties she had to go to in order to get it.

She had done things she hadn't been proud of, things that brought shame to her now.

She heard people clapping and looked up to see the mayor of Dundurn rising from his seat.

The mayor of Dundurn stood and addressed the residents.

"I've known Melvin Gourdeau for over twenty years. And in that time, I'd come to respect him. He was a man of principle and integrity. A simple man who thought of others before himself. He will be truly missed." The mayor walked back to his seat.

"I know every one of us has something positive to say about Mr. Gourdeau, but because of time, we'll only allow a few people."

A plump elderly woman got to her feet and walked to the front. She was dressed in a plain pink floral dress.

"You all know me. What you don't know is that Mr. Gourdeau came to my farm every morning to get the livestock. Never missed a day. And he refused to take anything in payment. Never known anyone like that in my entire life."

The woman walked back to her seat, and a young man took her place in front of the crowd.

"Fell off Betty last year and broke my ankle clear as day. I don't know what Mr. Gourdeau did, but I could walk a day after. God bless his soul."

The revving engine noise of a car pulled everyone's attention away from the memorial service. Gen looked through the barn window and saw a black sedan cruise to a stop a few meters from the barn. Gen turned her attention back to the young man, whom she recognized as Little Pete as the driver's door opened and a man got out.

Little Pete went back to his seat, and the minister beckoned Gen forward.

Gen walked to the minister's side and faced the crowd.

"Most of you knew him as Mr. Gourdeau or sir, but I knew him as my granddad. He was a rock in my life. He taught me everything I know, and I can boldly say that he was instrumental in what I am today. He is going to be missed dearly."

Gen took a deep breath and walked back to her seat.

She had so much more to say, but her throat felt clogged with unshed tears, and she wanted to remain strong.

Gen barely heard the words of praise from the other residents as she tried to get a handle on her emotions. She looked up in surprise when her mum tapped her on the shoulder, and she saw that the memorial service was over.

Gen nodded to her mum but remained in her seat. Her mum must have understood as she left Gen, and within seconds, the barn was empty.

Gen sat and looked at the portrait of her granddad.

She couldn't believe he was gone. The memorial service seemed to bring to stark reality the fact that she would never see him again.

A shadow passed her, but Gen's attention was on her grandfather's portrait. Her grandfather's smiling face brought a tear to her eye as she remembered his selfless service to everyone in the town.

Gen almost recoiled in shock when someone cleared his throat to get her attention.

Gen looked up into the eyes of a young man in his mid-thirties. He was clean-cut and handsome. He stood with his hands in his pocket, and Gen noticed that he stood out in his black suit and pants.

A city boy from his clothes, but Gen noticed that he carried himself with an easy confidence that was intimidating.

She knew the type. She had almost dated one on campus.

Gen frowned. His posture screamed military or any of the armed forces, and she wondered what he was doing here.

"Hello, sorry for your loss."

Gen got to her feet, feeling intimidated by his stature. He stood over six feet, lean muscled and athletic.

"Did you know my granddad?"

She still had to look up to meet his eyes.

"He was my client."

"Your client?"

Gen looked the stranger over.

What would granddad want with his sort?

"What kind of business would that be? You don't look like the average farmer."

The stranger laughed at Gen's comment.

"Definitely not farming."

The man's smile grated on Gen's nerves.

"That still doesn't answer the question."

"Client confidentiality. I'm just here to pay my respects."

"Well, since you've done that, I guess you can be on your way."

Gen was shocked by her response, but the stranger seemed to bring out the worst in her. And it didn't help that he exuded so much confidence.

They heard footsteps as someone approached the barn, and she turned.

A young man in a police uniform walked towards Gen.

Gen tried not to sigh as she watched Theo Cuttaham walk towards her. He was in his late twenties but still hadn't lost his boyish look. While that gave him a charming aspect, it made him seem like a kid playing pretend cop.

"Hey, Gen."

"Hey, Theo."

Theo turned and stared at the stranger.

Gen glared at Theo.

The stranger smiled and stretched out his hand to Theo.

"Hello. My name's Mark."

Theo was forced to shake Mark's hand, and Mark smiled, noticing Theo's reluctance.

There was an awkward silence, and they all stared at each other. The only one looking relaxed was Mark.

"He says he's granddad's business associate." Gen broke the silence.

"Huh."

Theo looked at Mark suspiciously.

"What type of business, if you don't mind my asking?" Theo had his thumbs tucked into his belt, trying to look intimidating.

Gen watched as Mark glanced at Theo and seemed to dismiss him as a threat. Gen couldn't shake the feeling that Mark was the predator in their midst.

"I'm in the security business. Mr. Gourdeau wanted me to watch over his property."

"Watch over the ranch? Triple 7?" Gen asked.

"That would be it," Mark agreed.

"Why?"

"That would be confidential," Mark said.

Gen gritted her teeth. It didn't make any sense.

Why would grandad want someone to watch the ranch? There was nothing of value. And why would he use an outside firm and not the police department in town?

"What did you say your name was?" Theo asked.

"Mark. Mark Reynolds." Mark dug into his breast pocket and brought out a business card. He handed the card to Theo.

"It was nice meeting you, Miss Isherwood." Mark nodded at her and left the barn.

"Who does he think he is?" Theo grumbled as Mark walked away.

Gen turned to head for the house as Theo reached for her hand.

"How are you coping? I know you and your granddad were very close."

"I'm okay, Theo. Thanks for asking."

Gen gently pulled her hand out of Theo's grasp.

It wasn't that she didn't like Theo. She had always seen him as the brother she never had. And that seemed to be the problem. She knew

Theo wanted more, but it had never seemed suitable.

"How long will you be staying?"

"Don't know yet. I deferred my program for a semester."

"So, you will be sticking around."

"I guess."

Theo walked beside Gen as she headed for the house. She noticed that Mark's car was gone. Theo's police van was parked close to the house, and they stopped by it.

"I'll check on you later today?" Theo asked.

"Sure."

Gen waved as Theo drove off.

The following two weeks passed in a blur for Gen.

She spent her time jogging because one thing that was cheap in Dundurn was solitude. She jogged along the deserted road, with only the occasional curious rodent poking its head out of holes or farmlands.

Theo had come as he had promised and had asked her out to dinner.

She had rejected Theo's offer but had asked for a raincheck.

She didn't want to hurt his feelings, but she also didn't want him to have any false hope that there would be anything between them.

Her mother had complained, but Gen had said it was her life and she would run it the way she wanted.

Gen breathed in and out in rhythm to her steps. She had always loved the outdoors and had been athletic in her time at the ranch. She passed picket fences and trees lining the roadside.

Going to university had changed all that.

Gen heard footsteps and looked behind her. Gen saw a figure jogging towards her and slowed her pace. Dundurn was a safe place, but she didn't recognize the person coming towards her. She relaxed when she saw that it was the city boy.

What had he said his name was again?

She watched Mark jogging towards her. He had on sweatpants and a polo shirt.

Gen was surprised to see him approaching, as she thought she was the only one on the road.

And what was he still doing in Dundurn? she wondered.

Mark gave her a nod of acknowledgment and jogged past her.

Gen increased her pace and passed him, nodding her head in his direction, a look of determination on her face.

This was her town. No city boy, or in this case, man, was going to take that from her.

Gen saw Mark catching up to her from the corner of her eyes and increased her pace. She felt her heart pounding and her breathing coming in a short burst.

She wasn't going to give up.

The road led to town, and Gen had marked a spot she used as her resting point. It was the gate to old Millar's abandoned shearing shed.

She was determined to beat Mark to that point.

She increased her pace again as she gave her all to reaching her resting point. Millar's gate loomed ahead of her.

She felt Mark gradually closing the gap she had created. Gen tried to increase her speed, but she was at her limit.

Mark caught up with her, and Gen glanced at him.

He had a look of complete focus on his face, and Gen understood that he must have realized she intended to stop at Millar's gate.

Gen felt her heart would explode from the pressure of pumping blood and oxygen into her veins.

Gen could see the gate. It was less than a hundred meters in front of her.

She needed just one more push, and Gen dug deep within herself. She felt like screaming as she pushed herself beyond her limit and reached the gate to Millar's farm a couple of meters ahead of Mark.

Gen fell to her knees in the sand and tried to inhale.

She felt lightheaded and knew she would pass out if she couldn't regulate her breathing.

That would just be annoying and ruin all her effort.

Mark got to her and knelt beside her.

"You need to take a deep breath, hold it for a second and release it through your mouth."

Gen thought of ignoring him, but her body was already responding.

She held her breath for a second and released it through her mouth. She struggled not to pass out and repeated the action.

Slowly, her heartbeat settled back to normal, and the pounding in her head reduced.

Gen glanced at Mark and realized he was close enough to touch. She could feel his breath on the nape of her neck, and she noticed that he wasn't out of breath.

Had he taken his own advice and quickly regulated his breathing, or had he not been trying to overtake her?

Mark must have read the expression on her face.

"Hey, you surprised me at the last leg. You won this."

Gen felt better with his reply and berated herself for it.

What did it matter if he acknowledged her efforts or not?

Gen noticed Mark studying her and raised an eyebrow.

"What?"

"You know, some people believe that they really know a person when they face them in combat," Mark said. "They believe that only in combat will your true nature emerge."

"So, are we in combat?"

"No, but you revealed a part of yourself that I find pleasantly surprising." Mark got to his feet and jogged back the way they had come.

Gen watched him go and frowned.

What was wrong with her? Gen realized she hadn't even bothered asking why he was still in Dundurn.

As Mark had gotten up, she had seen respect flicker in his eyes for a moment.

And she had been glad.

Gen knew she was going to pay for her reckless action as she dragged herself back to the house.

Her legs felt like two thick pillars that she had to drag behind her.

She walked into the ranch but headed to the barn.

She might as well abuse her body by pounding on the anvil.

She had moved the anvil back to its position sometime after the memorial service. Gen looked at the hammer, and it seemed to call to her.

Gen picked the hammer up and wondered if she shouldn't be in a hot bathtub right now, soaking all the aches away.

She really didn't have to do this.

But she needed to think, and this was her way of focusing.

She swung the hammer down.

She couldn't deny that she felt drawn to Mark.

There was chemistry there, but that didn't mean she had to dive right in, did it?

She barely knew him, no, scratch that. She didn't know him at all.

She had only seen him twice, and she felt attracted to him.

And why was he here anyway?

It didn't make sense that granddad would hire him to watch the ranch.

What was he watching out for?

Dundurn was a small town, and everybody knew everybody.

The ranch didn't have anything of value.

The only thing of value to her was the people living on the ranch.

Could he have…?

Gen missed a swing and hit the edge of the anvil. She grunted in pain as the anvil tilted from the force of the strike.

Gen dropped the hammer and bent to take a closer look at the anvil.

The nail holding the anvil to the stump had pulled out of the stump.

Great.

She would need to remove the nail and set the anvil aright.

Gen retrieved a pincer from the set of tools and tried to pull out the nail.

She grunted with effort as the nail refused to come out.

Grunting in irritation, Gen gripped the nail to shake it loose.

The world bent.

N

CHAPTER SIX

A groan of anguish spun Gen around.

She gazed in wonder at her surroundings. She wasn't in Dundurn, that was for sure.

The air felt drier, particles swirling in the air as a slight breeze blew.

Someone came out of the haze created by the dust, and Gen staggered backwards.

The man passed by Gen. He was wearing armor plating that looked like chainmail.

Was that…a Roman soldier?

Where was she?

Gen followed the man and found the source of the groan she had heard.

A figure lay on a wooden cross. His wrists were impaled to the cross by thick nails.

Gen realized where she was.

Golgotha.

It couldn't be.

The man groaned in anguish as Gen heard a pounding noise. She slowly looked down to the foot of the cross where a soldier was bent over, a crude hammer in his hand.

Embedded in the feet of the man on the cross was a nail.

The soldier drove his hammer down, and Gen turned away, feeling the cry of the figure on the cross penetrating her soul.

No!

Gen looked around helplessly.

What could she do?

It seemed she was a spectator to a crucifixion.

Could it be who she thought it was?

Gen recalled some of the stories her granddad had told her, and she looked around. She saw the crowd gathered some meters away and the wailing of some of the women in the crowd. The soldier continued hitting the nail, and the sound reverberated within her. She covered her ears as she tried to shut out the sound of pain and anguish.

She was witnessing the crucifixion of Jesus Christ.

I see you!

It was a whisper but filled with malice and hate. Gen looked around but didn't see anybody.

I see you, harbinger, daughter of doom and destruction.

The voice surrounded her, sucking her into an endless void of darkness and gloom.

Gen gasped.

She looked around in confusion.

Where was she? She touched her face and realized it was wet with tears. The loft of the barn filled her vision.

She was back.

Gen slowly picked herself up from the floor of the barn.

Had she passed out?

Had she been hallucinating?

Was she tripping?

No, she had stopped taking molly. And it had looked so real, more like a vision than a hallucination.

Gen stared at the nail on the stump.

Could…could it be the same nail? A nail that crucified Jesus? Was that even possible? What was the nail doing here in her granddad's barn, among his tools?

There was only one way to be sure, and Gen stretched out her hand slowly to the nail on the stump.

Her hand hovered over the nail, and she felt a slight vibration around it.

This was no ordinary nail.

Gen took a deep breath and grasped the nail, shuddering as she was transported again.

She was back in Golgotha, but the scene was different. Gen could see three crosses on the hilltop. It looked like she was in an encampment or what passed as one. Gen watched as four soldiers crouched around a small mound of clothes.

They spoke harshly, jostling and pushing each other. Gen couldn't make out their features, as they wore similar garb and helmets, but one was bulkier than the others.

One of the soldiers finally got up and brought out a little cup and shook it. A rattling sound filled the air, and the other soldiers looked to be in agreement with whatever they had planned.

The soldier shook the cup again and threw the contents on the ground. They all leaned in, and Gen watched the proceedings.

A pair of crudely shaped dice caused the rattling sound.

One of the soldiers clapped in joy and snatched a piece of fine cloth from the floor. The soldier who had brought out the cup pulled out a knife, but the winner was faster. The tip of his sword pointed at the cupbearer's throat.

The cupbearer didn't move, and the other two soldiers sputtered as they tried to diffuse the tension.

Gen could not make out a word that was being said. Still, she heard the soldier standing by the winner repeatedly say, "Lucilius."

Must be his name, Gen thought.

She knew this scene. It had been recorded in the Bible.

This was the story about the four soldiers who had cast a lot for Jesus's robe because they hadn't wanted to tear the robe into pieces.

It was real.

While she believed in the Bible's authenticity, it was another thing entirely to live through one minute of it.

Gen watched as the soldiers parted, and the winner took the robe and shoved it into his knapsack.

Then, he looked straight at Gen.

I see you! You cannot hide from me, nail bearer.

Gen released her hand from the nail and returned to the present. This was the nail — the nail that was used to crucify Jesus Christ. And why did that voice fill her with dread? And what did it mean when he called her 'nail bearer?'

Had her granddad known?

Was this the precious item he had hired Mark to protect?

Why hadn't he said anything to her?

Thoughts spun in her head until Gen felt she was going to collapse from the pounding.

Gen cleared the area around the anvil and stump and gently moved both to a corner of the workspace.

She needed to think about the next step.

Who could she tell, and would they believe her? She couldn't just walk up to someone and say she had the nail that crucified Jesus. She would be ridiculed and scorned. Probably end up in a psychiatric ward.

No one would believe her unless she was able to convince them.

Touching the nail would convince anybody, though.

Gen shut the barn behind her and walked to the house.

N

CHAPTER SEVEN

Mark stepped out of the shower with a towel draped around his waist.

Gen had surprised him today.

He had taken the assignment because he was bored and felt a change of scenery would be ideal for him. His last protection gig hadn't gone as smoothly as he would have liked.

He had been tasked with protecting the daughter of a whistleblower. The father had planned to testify against a pharmaceutical company. He had been with the young woman for two weeks as the case had developed in court. The close proximity must have made the woman begin to have feelings for him — emotions he had not been able to reciprocate. The woman had felt scorned and had run away one night.

Mark had been able to track her down but couldn't stop her from asking for another bodyguard. Her father had agreed, and someone else had been called in, but the woman had been found dead two days later.

Mark remembered the distraught look on the father's face when he had come to his office begging for retribution. He had wanted revenge, but Mark had to tell him that his company only dealt in extractions and protection. He wasn't in the revenge business.

The father was hurt and disillusioned, and Mark had felt his pain. Against his better judgment, he had tracked down the killer who had taken the life of the man's daughter.

After that job, he had needed a break and the chance to relax. The opportunity to watch over a ranch and its owners had come soon after. This seemed like the kind of job he needed at the moment. It was easy money. Watch the girl and, by extension, her parents. That seemed easy enough, especially in a town where nothing happened.

He had run a background check on Mr. Gourdeau and Genesis Isherwood.

Mr. Gourdeau had inherited the ranch from his father and had run a stud farm for horses for some years. Things had not worked out well, and Mr. Gourdeau had kept the ranch as a home for his daughter and granddaughter instead.

When he had agreed to take the job, he had scouted the 'Triple 7' ranch and its surroundings. There had been no sinister basement full of explosive devices or young girls locked up against their wishes. The place had been clean.

Mr. Gourdeau's background had been clean too, but short. Records showed that the Gourdeaus had been in the town for generations. Mark had dug deeper and had found out that the records had been forged.

Mark had chosen not to dig too deep, though. There could be several reasons why Mr. Gourdeau had fake records of his family tree. He may be hiding some sinister dark secret, but Mark felt it wasn't his job to judge a man by his ancestry. Mr. Gourdeau had a clean record. He was a beloved citizen of Dundurn and had a loving family. The only other person of interest was his granddaughter.

Genesis. A peculiar name.

Nothing much had come up about her, but Genesis's social network had shown an extroverted, party-going girl.

That wasn't strange, but the last couple of years seemed to have been difficult for her. She seemed to have mixed with the wrong crowd and may have developed a minor drug habit. Again, that wasn't a crime. Mark had interviewed Gen's roommate, and she had described Genesis as a caring and loving person who would go out of her way to help strangers. He had hacked her social media accounts and email and had seen emails from her family and friends.

There had been messages from friends concerned about her and the direction she had been heading.

Her parents had corresponded regularly with her, but that had stopped a year after Genesis was admitted to university. She had stopped replying to her parents' emails, and the only messages she had sent said she was stressed from her workload.

Mark had come to Dundurn expecting to see a spoilt and pampered girl.

But Genesis had surprised him.

The jog that morning had been a glimpse of the actual Genesis, and he had been impressed.

She had been determined.

This was something Mark could relate to.

His drill sergeant would have been glad to have Genesis on the team. Mark's cellphone buzzed on the bed, and he picked it up.

"Hello."

"Hello. Is this Mark Reynolds?"

"Yes, it is."

"This is Gen Isherwood. We met at my granddad's memorial. Theo gave me your number."

"How may I help you, Miss Isherwood?"

"Eh...could you come to the ranch?"

"Is there a problem?"

"Oh, no. Not at all," Gen quickly reassured. "But there's something I need to know, and eh... I thought you could help..."

"You need to know about what?"

"Can't say over the phone, but I thought you could help."

"I'll be there in an hour."

"Great. See you then."

Mark frowned as he dropped the phone and pulled on some clothes. He played the conversation back in his mind as he analyzed it and looked for any sign to show she was in danger.

Her voice had sounded...excited?

Gen groaned as she dropped her phone on the kitchen table.

What could have possessed her to call Mark? She barely knew him.

Why hadn't she called Theo over instead? There had been ample chance to invite him over when she called to ask for Mark's number. He had wanted to know what was going on and why she wanted Mark's number.

Gen had told him it had to do with granddad's stuff, and while it was technically accurate, Theo had sensed that there was more to it than that.

She had heard the hurt in his voice and could have reassured him, but she had kept quiet. She had been close to Theo as a kid but going to the university had changed her. It wasn't that she felt she was better than him or that she was too good for him. She liked him as a friend and valued that friendship, but she didn't want anything to jeopardize that friendship.

Gen went to her room to take a shower and wait for Mark.

Gen sat on a chair by the porch when Mark drove into the ranch in his flashy black sedan, and Gen shook her head.

He must stand out like a nun in a den full of thieves.

She grimaced to think of what the town folks would think of a stranger paying a visit to the 'Triple 7' ranch.

Well, that boat has sailed, she thought to herself.

Maybe she was impulsive, but it had felt right.

She watched as Mark walked towards her. He wore blue jeans with a black T-shirt, and Gen noted that he glanced around quickly as he approached.

Was he checking the area?

Definitely military. Gen was going for Special Forces…or maybe Commando…or better still, the Navy Seals.

Mark got to the porch, and Gen stood up.

"So, what did you call me about?"

"You'll see, but we have to go to the barn over there."

Mark followed Gen's hand with his eyes and saw the barn. He turned his attention back to Gen after sizing up their destination.

"I know it was kinda sudden, but I needed a second opinion."

Mark took the remark in his stride and waited.

Not one for idle chitchat, is he? Gen thought and stifled a smile.

They walked to the barn in silence, but Gen felt relaxed. She didn't feel the need to fill the silence with idle conversation.

Gen pulled the anvil and stump from where she hid it to the center of the workspace.

"I need you to do something for me," she said, dusting the dirt off her hands.

Mark stood by her side in silence, but again, she noted that he had covered the area as they walked in. Gen could feel Mark beside her even though he didn't invade her personal space.

"I need you to grab that nail for me." Gen pointed to the nail holding the anvil to the stump.

Mark looked at the anvil and then at Gen.

He couldn't comprehend what angle she was playing.

From their jog earlier today, Mark didn't think Gen was a prankster.

But then again, how well did he really know her?

Mark studied the anvil.

It was old and tilted at an angle due to the nail protruding from the wood.

The same nail Gen had told him to grab.

Was it connected to cables that would shock him?

But that line of thinking meant she purposely wanted to hurt him, and he couldn't see any reason why.

"Just grab the nail and tell me what you think," Gen said in exasperation.

Taking a deep breath, Mark hunched his shoulders and grabbed the nail.

Gen watched as Mark bent down to grab hold of the nail.

Her heart pounded as though a thousand tiny birds were trapped inside it, and she prepared herself to grab him in case he stumbled or passed out.

Gen stared in shock as Mark stood upright.

Nothing happened!

She stared at Mark and then at the nail.

"Did you grab it firmly enough?"

Mark frowned and looked at her suspiciously.

"Did you?"

"Yeah, I did."

"And?"

"It felt like a nail. A bit rusty and cold."

"No, no, no."

Gen squatted by the stump and stretched her hand out.

She immediately felt her fingers tingle from what felt like a static current.

"What's wrong, Miss Isherwood?"

"Nothing."

Mark frowned again but kept silent. He watched as Gen's hand shook as it hovered over the nail. *What was unique about the nail?*

Mark heard a sound and spun around; a small blade appeared in his right palm.

Gen looked up towards the sound of footsteps. She noticed Mark had blocked her view by stepping in front of her. She stood up and looked around him to see Theo standing by the barn door and saw Mark slipping something shiny into a sheath on his belt.

Was that a knife?

"Hi, Theo," Gen said.

Gen stood up and tried not to look guilty. She hadn't been doing anything wrong, but the glance Theo gave her and Mark seemed to say otherwise.

"Just checking to see if you're all right, Gen. There's a report of a wild cougar in this vicinity. I'm informing everyone in the neighborhood."

"I'm good, Theo, but thanks for the heads-up."

Gen noticed Theo eye Mark rudely, but Mark ignored the gesture. Mark moved towards the door, and Gen saw the corner of his lips lift in amusement.

Gen walked Mark and Theo out of the barn and shut the door. She brought out a padlock from her pocket and locked the barn.

"Anyone up for some lemonade?"

"I'll pass," Mark responded.

He walked to his car as Gen led Theo to the house.

❖

Mark crept slowly through the field at the back of 'Triple 7' ranch. The moon's half crescent allowed Mark to see a horse grazing near the barn.

He barely made a sound as he advanced. The air filled with sounds of frogs croaking and crickets chirping as he made his way silently towards the barn.

Light from the house could be seen, and Mark guessed the occupants would soon retire for the night.

He had come prepared for this reconnaissance. He had on dark military gear and wore a helmet with night vision. He wasn't expecting trouble, but he preferred being prepared.

Genesis had acted strangely in the barn. The nail on the anvil meant something to her, and he was going to find out what that was. He had thought about the incident in the barn earlier in the day and figured Gen was hiding something. He got to the barn door without incident and knelt beside the padlock.

The lock wasn't even worth bothering over.

This was the back end of civilization, so no one expected someone like him stalking the night.

Mark pulled out a pair of picklock tools and inserted them into the padlock. He rotated the picks until he heard a clicking sound. The padlock opened silently, and Mark gently pulled open the door. He slid through the narrow gap he created and shut the door behind him.

The anvil and stump stood where he had seen it earlier in the day, and he advanced slowly towards it.

Why had Genesis been fascinated by the nail? He had seen her hand shaking when she stretched it towards the nail, as though she expected something to happen.

Mark brought out a Geiger counter from his pocket and checked around the anvil and stump for radiation. The counter clicked as Mark moved it over the anvil and stump, but the indicator read nothing.

He remembered Genesis had been weary around the anvil, but he couldn't tell if it was from anything emitting from the anvil or from fear.

Mark pulled off the glove on his right hand and slowly stretched it towards the nail on the stump. His hand hovered over the nail as he tried to get a read on it.

Nothing.

He remembered Genesis's face when he had said he hadn't felt anything.

She had been distraught.

Mark took a deep breath and placed his hand on the nail.

Nothing.

He was missing something here.

He grabbed the nail and pulled it, but the nail didn't budge. He applied more pressure, but the nail remained stuck in the stump.

Mark looked around and saw a pair of pincers. He grabbed the pincers and gripped the nail.

His muscles flexed as he tried to pry the nail out of the stump.

What the...

Mark grabbed the pincers with both arms and tugged with all his might.

The nail remained in the same position.

He tried twisting the nail sideways, but the nail refused to move from its position.

Mark stared at the nail.

What the heck is going on here?

Mark found a hammer and targeted the center of the nail with the hammer's head. He took a deep breath and swung at it with all his strength.

A loud clang rang across the barn, and Mark looked at the nail.

The nail remained as it was.

Mark's arms throbbed from the force of the blow, and he could see an indention in the hammer from the head of the nail.

He couldn't believe his eyes. This wasn't an ordinary nail.

Gen was about to switch off her bedside lamp when she heard a loud clanging sound. She paused and listened.

The sound had come from the barn.

Silence filled the room, but Gen was sure she had heard the clanging sound. She got her coat and left her bedroom. She considered waking her dad but decided not to.

This was Dundurn. What could possibly go wrong?

Maybe the raccoon Theo had warned her about was in the barn.

Gen held a torch in her hand as she approached the barn. She saw the padlock hanging on the barn door, and looking both ways, she slowly crept in.

❖

Gen entered the barn, and Mark silently moved behind her.

With a quick glance, he covered her mouth with his hand and whispered into her ear.

"Don't scream. It's me."

Gen tensed in his arms as a scream subsided in her chest, and Mark relaxed his hold on her. Suddenly, Gen drove her head back and slammed Mark in the face.

Mark grunted in pain but held on to Gen.

"It's Mark!"

He quickly released her but got ready to react if she screamed.

Gen turned and glared at Mark as he removed his night goggles.

"What are you doing here at this time of night?!" Gen whispered harshly.

Gen rubbed the back of her head as she moved and switched on the light.

She saw Mark's army camouflage and raised an eyebrow.

"Don't get it wrong, but I came to check on that," Mark nodded towards the nail in the stump. "You looked worried this morning, so I decided to see if there was anything to it."

Gen folded her arms across her chest and continued to glare at him. "And it couldn't wait till morning?"

"I needed to know if it was a threat or not. I have been charged with your safety. But I found the strangest thing."

Mark walked to the anvil, and Gen followed. She still couldn't decide if Mark could be trusted.

She watched as Mark bent and tried to pull the nail out of the stump. The nail remained stuck in the stump.

"It's stuck."

"Exactly," Mark picked up the hammer and showed Gen the indent on the head.

"See this? I tried to hammer the nail back in."

Gen looked at the hammer and frowned.

"You are saying the nail did that?"

"I can strike it again, Miss Isherwood."

Mark raised the hammer as Gen held his arm.

"I heard the sound before and since you're sneaking around in my granddad's barn, I think we're beyond being so informal. Call me Gen."

"Gen."

Gen smiled inwardly. She liked the way her name sounded when he said it. Giving herself a mental shake, she concentrated on the scene before her.

Gen was wary about the feeling she got from the nail, but she bent and extended her hand towards it. Taking a deep breath, she grasped the nail and pulled it.

Gen staggered and fell on her rear with the nail in her hand.

There had been no flashbacks or visions.

"What the heck is going on here?!"

"I should be asking you that. Did you swap the nail? Is that why you snuck in here?"

Mark defensively raised his hands.

"Why would I do that, Miss Isher...err, Gen?"

"I don't know. Why are you sneaking around the place at this time of the night?"

"I told you earlier. Your grandfather tasked me..."

"To keep me, the ranch, and my family safe," Gen completed his sentence, rolling her eyes.

Mark sighed at Gen's flippant remark before saying, "Hold on a minute. Put the nail back."

Gen looked at him distrustfully but obeyed. She shoved the nail hard into the hole in the stump of wood.

Mark bent, grabbed the nail, and pulled.

Gen watched as Mark grunted, trying to pull out the nail.

"Are you kidding me? What are you up to, Mr. Reynolds?"

"At this rate, I think you can also call me Mark," Mark smiled as drops of perspiration glistened on his forehead, but Gen only glared at him.

He had to be faking it. He was up to something...

Gen stepped back as Mark picked up the hammer and, in one smooth motion, slammed it on the nail. A crack filled the barn as the head of the hammer broke off and flew across the barn.

Gen turned in the direction the broken hammer head had gone and was glad she had released the horses to roam the ranch.

"What just happened?" Gen asked.

Even if the hammer had a fracture, it should have driven the nail deep into the stump of wood. That could only mean one thing.

Her visions were genuine. She was staring at the nail used to crucify Jesus Christ.

❖

The staccato sound of high heels on the marble floor filled the hallway as a young woman smartly dressed in a business suit stopped before a door.

She smoothed non-existent creases from her dress as she waited by the door.

A sucking sound echoed as the metal doors parted, and the woman then entered.

The interior was dimly lit but not too dark to make seeing difficult. She walked in confidently with an aura of elegance surrounding her. The sound of her heels was muted on the thick rug that covered the floor of the executive office.

The woman stopped before a glass desk and waited as the executive chair spun around, revealing her employer.

"We have confirmation of the item you require, sir."

Her employer leaned forward and moved out of the shadows cast by the dimly lit room. She shivered as her employer looked at her. He seemed in his mid-fifties with a lean, athletic look.

"Well done, Miss Paige."

The woman made a hasty retreat from the room.

Her employer steepled his hands and leaned back in his chair as a smile plastered itself across his face. His handsome features were marred by a scar that ran across his face — a scar that had damaged one of his eyes. The damaged eye looked milky, as though it had cataracts.

N

CHAPTER EIGHT

JERUSALEM 327 A.D.

Empress Helena staggered back.

She looked around her, trying to get her bearings. She was in a lonely alley, and the only sound was a startled cat's spitting. Helena couldn't blame the cat. She felt the same fear as she stared at the man who had done the impossible. She wasn't in the cavern anymore, but from the commotion she could still hear, she wasn't far from the church that was being constructed.

The alley was fenced on both sides by brick walls, and Helena saw that the alley ended in another street. Light poured from the street, but Helena knew that any hope of getting away from the man beside her was futile.

The elderly man, Merlin, as he had called himself, took a deep breath to steady himself, and Helena took one step back. She clutched her discovery tight to her chest as she wondered what was to become of her.

"You need not fear me, Empress Helena. I mean you no harm."

"Then why take me away from my guard and from the help that was arriving?"

"Calisto will make do. His path doesn't end there. And the help you sought wasn't the help that came. You would have lost that to the enemy," Merlin said, pointing at the nails in Helena's hands.

"What do you know about these?"

"Enough. We share a common goal."

"And what is that?"

"To stop the end of the world that the enemy seeks to bring about."

Helena looked at Merlin warily. She couldn't decide if she needed to fear him or not. He still exuded power, and this display of translocation was no mere feat.

She had heard that only practitioners of magic and summoners of celestial beings could perform such a feat but had discarded these stories

51

as figments of deluded imaginations and those who had imbibed too much wine.

Now it seemed she would be classed in such a position, for who would believe what she had seen?

"We cannot remain here. What you hold will draw the accursed here like a moth to a flame. We must hide."

"Hide? Why do I have to hide? I'm sure by now, guards from the palace will have come to my aid. I say we head to the palace."

Merlin sighed, unable to explain to Helena what danger they were in.

"You will have to trust me, your highness. The enemy's reach is far, and safety is only of the Lord. We will stay out of their reach till we can make sense of our situation and predicament."

"Our? I see no place where we come…"

Merlin heard a sound and spun around. A little boy holding a stick figure stood at the entrance of the alley. The boy stopped in fear as he sensed the danger he had stumbled upon. Merlin frowned and turned back to Empress Helena.

"We are exposed here. You must make a choice now. Come with me and live or try on your own and perish."

He turned and walked towards the little boy who still stood rooted to the spot at the mouth of the alley. Merlin sighed in relief and quietly smiled when he heard Empress Helena's footsteps hurry to catch up with him.

Calisto groaned in pain and staggered to his feet. The wound on his side had stopped bleeding but was still raw from the magic that had saved his life. He looked around and saw the remaining two guards rush to his side.

Immediately a band of soldiers swarmed the cavern and surrounded Calisto and his guards. A centurion strode calmly into the room, his helmet under his armpit, and he regarded the room with disdain.

Calisto recognized the centurion immediately — *Gaius Octavius* — a man rising rapidly in the political arena of Rome. A close friend to Marcus Livinus, who had the ear of an influential senator. Calisto watched as Gaius surveyed the cavern. A group of soldiers gathered around the assassin, who had stopped whimpering and knelt on the floor, and Calisto watched from a distance.

"My name is…"

"I know who you are, soldier." Calisto frowned. Something about Gaius Octavius was off. He had seen the man a couple of times when he lobbied Empress Helena for resources to fund his private predilection for wine.

Calisto saw the twitch in Octavius's eye, and his frown deepened. He made eye contact with his guards, and they immediately assumed a relaxed but guarded stance.

"Arrest the traitor," Octavius blurted.

The soldiers surrounding the assassin moved closer to the man.

"Not him, you goats. Him!"

Octavius pulled out his sword and pointed at Calisto. The soldiers seemed bewildered by Octavius's command. The two guards beside Calisto pulled out their swords and stepped forward with their weapons lowered and ready.

Blood would be spilled soon.

"On what charge, Centurion?" Calisto noted that Octavius looked uncomfortable as Octavius fidgeted on his feet and kept looking behind him in the direction of the downed assassin.

"You are found guilty of conspiracy to overthrow the empire and causing instability by killing the Empress Mother."

"That is preposterous, and no one would believe you. I live to serve Empress Helena."

What madness had overtaken Octavius? And what was off about him?

It came to Calisto in a flash.

There was one meeting with Empress Helena when Octavius had been drunk, having consumed more wine than he was accustomed to. Calisto had stood and watched him rant and rave for an increase in the pittance he believed Empress Helena was giving him.

He had held his goblet all the while he ranted. And his goblet had been...

Calisto noticed that Octavius carried his sword in his right hand, the opposite hand he had used throughout that meeting. A tiny detail, but Calisto recalled he signed the document Empress Helena had presented with his left hand, his dominant hand.

"Who are you?" Calisto asked Octavius.

For a moment, Octavius looked startled and moved back defensively. He seemed all wrong to Calisto, and Octavius's fear was a damning factor. The real Octavius was proud and sarcastic, looking at the rest of humanity from a lofty position of nobility and privilege.

"Enough of this mindless chatter. Kill the fool, Remus. Kill them all." The assassin pushed the soldiers around him aside and walked to Octavius's side.

"What took you so long?" he asked.

Octavius grimaced.

"This body took some getting used to. It was also quite inconvenient getting rid of the original body."

The assassin grunted and stared at Calisto.

Calisto saw that one of the assassin's eyes was red and watery, and he had a thin wound on his face caused by the nail.

"You do not look too good, assassin. And I take it this imposter standing before me isn't the real Gaius Octavius." Calisto noted the silence that followed his declaration.

"Too bad. I was never really fond of the fool, but it saves me having to feel guilty."

The assassin seemed weakened somehow, and Calisto saw the opportunity to end the fight. He snatched a short knife from the guard standing by his side.

All his guards carried knives for bloody work in close quarters. In a matter of seconds, he jumped to his side and stabbed the nearest soldier in the throat and took his sword from his limp hand. In the same motion, he swung at the next soldier, who tried to deflect the blow.

The soldiers were probably good in their own right, but they faced the Praetorian guard's leader — the undefeated champion of the arena.

The soldiers saw their end coming, and they clenched in despair. Calisto used the flat of his blade to strike at vital organs or sensitive parts. He aimed to disable and not kill. His two guards followed his lead, breaking bones and incapacitating soldiers as they wove through the rank and headed towards the assassin and the imposter.

Calisto watched in surprise as the imposter raised a bow and drew an arrow, but he deflected the aim with the flat of his blade. He saw the imposter release another arrow, and he swung low. The arrow whisked over his head, and he heard a grunt behind him.

Calisto spun as a soldier came at him with a thrust. He slapped the flat end of his blade at the soldier's head, and the man crumbled on the ground with his blood spurting onto the sand. Calisto saw one of his guards holding the end of an arrow protruding from his shoulder and breaking the shaft. The second guard was breathing heavily.

Calisto looked at the imposter and the assassin. *So close.* Calisto could end them both here, but one thing the Colosseum had drilled into him was care for his brethren, in this case, his guards.

Calisto rushed to the cavern entrance, and the soldiers there parted for him and his guards. In moments, they were out of the cavern and on the busy streets.

Empress Helena watched as Merlin entered a house, and then she followed. She was still suspicious of the man who had saved her life. It couldn't be by chance that this stranger had been at the cavern and had the powers he had displayed. Helena wondered if she was a fool to trust the man, but her instincts hadn't screamed for her to run.

The house she entered was small, with a table occupying the center of the room. A man greeted Merlin, and they exchanged words too faint for Helena to hear. Helena looked around, noting the crumbling walls and cracked floor. The house didn't look lived in.

He looked like a native of the land with his tanned leathery skin and long locks of hair emerging from beneath the turban he wore.

"This way." Merlin beckoned for her to follow.

There was a narrow corridor that led to a narrower staircase. Merlin took the flight of stairs swiftly, unconcerned for his safety. Helena stopped by the stairs. Calisto would have been the first to check the environment for signs of danger or hostility in situations like this. He would have told her in a stern voice to remain guarded while he checked to see if it was safe.

Helena realized that she missed him and his stability and certainty. He was a rock that weathered and sheltered her from any storm.

Merlin popped his head over the stair railing and beckoned for her to come up the stairs.

Empress Helena sighed. It seemed improbable that Merlin would save her life and then look for a derelict house to end it. If he wanted to take the nails from her, Helena did not doubt that he could. Not that she wouldn't put up a fight. She may be old, but she still had a few surprises left in her.

Helena sighed again and climbed the stairs, unsure of what to do next, so she decided to wait and see what would happen. The wood creaked in protest, and Helena wondered if she was making the right decision.

Merlin had hinted that their objectives aligned. What was her objective? She had come to Jerusalem under the direction of a vision she had had.

She reached the top of the staircase and took a moment to regain her breath as she noticed the room Merlin had entered on her right. She could see it had a small cot and a stool in a corner.

Helena entered, looked at the cot, and then at Merlin.

"This is so that we can talk without interruptions. Also, the house is warded so that Lucilius and his friends won't be able to detect the nails you carry."

"Is Lucilius the one that came to the cavern?"

"Yes. Lucilius has been looking for the nails for quite a while now."

"Why?"

"Because he has to. What you hold, Empress Helena, will change the world. But great are your adversaries. Four men are on the hunt for these nails. Of these, Lucilius, you have met. The others are Atticus, Remus, and Marius. It is my duty to guard the bearer of the nails."

"And what about me? What am I to do next?"

"We must find a way to protect the nails. To do that, you must grow in spirit and faith. I know you have had a trying period with the death of your grandson."

Helena bit her lip to stop herself from snapping at Merlin. She shied away from the topic of her grandson, Crispus. His death was still fresh in her mind and caused pain in her heart. Crispus was also one of the reasons she was in Jerusalem.

She had needed to get away from the politics of Rome. The visions had started, and Helena had decided on a pilgrimage to some holy sites. Helena sat on the small cot and rested her back against the wall.

"How do I do that? Grow in spirit and faith? What does it entail? Is this a new philosophy or religion?" Helena brought herself back to the present and her current dilemma.

Someone wanted the nails and was willing to kill to get their hands on them.

Merlin raised his hands in a calming manner. He could see that Helena was agitated, and he couldn't blame her. He probably would have reacted in a worse way if told that the fate of humanity rested in his hands.

"You believe in the Son of God, the Messiah of humankind. You profess to be a disciple of Jesus the Nazarene. All I'm saying is that you need to know Him more to be imbued with His power."

"Power? And why would I need His power? I am Empress Mother to the greatest emperor in the world."

"But you fight an entity many times stronger. This battle is not of the flesh but of the spirit. The enemy has many followers, and you need to be strong so that he doesn't have a hold on you."

Empress Helena listened and pondered on Merlin's words in the silence that followed.

She had seen a vision of the cross, had felt the power in the nails. Even now, as they lay on her lap, she could feel it calling out.

"What must I do to know Him better?"

Merlin smiled.

"That part isn't as difficult as it seems. I can tell you my experience, and maybe that will guide you."

Calisto looked around.

They needed to get off the streets, as they were attracting unwanted attention. Calisto reduced his pace to a crawl and tried to be as inconspicuous as he could. They had found an alley to remove the arrow from the injured guard's shoulder.

What was going on? Calisto wondered.

A centurion that wasn't a centurion. An assassin sent to kill the Empress Mother. Calisto understood the nature of politics played by the members of the senate, but this felt wrong. Nobody would be foolhardy enough to try and kill Empress Helena.

Unless the person had absolute power?

Who else but Emperor Constantine? But Calisto knew without a shadow of a doubt that it couldn't be Emperor Constantine.

That left very few people.

If they planned to assassinate Empress Helena and create chaos, Calisto swore to make it his sole ambition to thwart their plans.

But first, he needed to find Empress Helena.

He had taken a gamble entrusting the empress's safety to a stranger, but at that moment, it had seemed the best choice since he thought that death had been imminent.

"Brothers, we need to split up. Head back to the palace and wait for me. I have to find the empress."

The guards nodded.

Calisto continued in the direction he had been going while the guards turned the other way. They would split again when convenient to make it difficult to be tracked.

Empress Helena sat on the small cot and watched Merlin talking with the owner of the house. She couldn't make out the words, but the man nodded and left the room.

"What did you tell him?" she asked. Merlin looked at her and smiled.

"I asked him to get an item for me."

Helena decided not to push the matter further. She had decided to trust this magician, and he hadn't proven himself false so far. Merlin sat on the stool and placed his hands on his thigh.

Helena pondered their last discussion about the nails and knowing God better. She already had an inclination about that, as she had taken to

57

Christianity some time back. Her son Constantine had played an instrumental part in her decision to leave behind her false gods and serve the Almighty. Her son's adamant faith in God had been like a shining beacon of hope for her to see and emulate.

She knew the Christians were persecuted, and only her position as Empress Mother kept her safe from some of the men's devices in her son's council. They frowned on the emperor's beliefs and felt his plans to grant amnesty to Christians to be wrong.

That was why her son's decision to execute Crispus didn't make any sense to her.

Grimacing, she adjusted her dress and looked at Merlin. He sat by the wall and had his eyes closed. He seemed to be meditating, and Helena envied the calm look on his face.

How can one get to know God better?

She had attended meetings where disciples taught God's word and how their experiences with God had marked their lives. She remembered one such meeting. She had disguised herself so that she didn't attract unwanted attention and had sat with a mixed crowd of different nationalities and races.

There had been a sense of peace in that meeting. The words the disciple had preached had brought peace to her heart.

The meeting had been about love. Love for God and love for our neighbors, and the disciple had gone to great lengths explaining who our neighbor was. He had talked about the good Samaritan parable, saying it was the same parable that Jesus had taught the multitude. The good Samaritan had seen a wounded man by the roadside and had helped him. Helena had taken the parable to heart and had tried to live by that mantra.

Helena coughed, and Merlin opened his eyes.

"What do we do next, magician?"

"We wait."

"Wait for what?"

"For our host to return."

Helena frowned as she waited for Merlin to elaborate.

"A lot of people will come after those nails, so it's best if we hide them."

"And how do we do that?"

Helena heard footsteps and turned to see the host come back, carrying a metal contraption.

"What is this?"

"How we hide it… in plain sight."

Merlin took the anvil from the man and placed it in a corner.

CHAPTER NINE

The early morning sunlight filtered into the kitchen as Gen and Mark sat by the kitchen table with the nail from the anvil resting on the table between them.

Mark had gone home the night before in bewilderment, his mind still refusing to accept what he had seen at the barn.

He didn't notice that Gen looked beautiful in a white-lace top and jeans.

Okay, so he did realize that the sun seemed to catch her face and give it a surreal look that he found enticing.

Mark picked up the cup beside him and realized it was empty.

"Let me get this straight. When you touch the nail, you get a vision."

Gen nodded.

"But you seem to be the only one who can see these visions."

"Well, between the two of us."

"And you don't know why that is so?"

"One thing we do know with certainty is that this is no ordinary nail. We both agree on that."

Mark nodded. His shoulder still felt sore from the force exerted.

"And my visions, if they are real and my heart tells me that they are, are of the crucifixion of Jesus Christ."

"Jesus Christ! The same one Christians worship?"

"The very same. And from your tone, I take it that you're not a believer."

Mark looked down at his empty cup of coffee.

"Let's just say that in my line of work, I've seen some terrible things done by His followers."

"Hey, the fact that there are some bad eggs doesn't make every Christian bad."

"And your point being?"

"What He is and what He stands for hasn't changed."

"And what is He?"

Gen looked at Mark and gestured to the nail.

They heard a sound and looked up when Gen's mother entered the kitchen.

"Oh, you didn't say you had a visitor, Genesis."

"Good morning, Mum."

"Hello, Mrs. Isherwood."

"Hello. Who are you?"

"My name is Mark Reynolds."

'He worked for granddad, Mum."

'Oh?"

"Granddad wanted Mark to help him with some legal advice."

Gen's mum smiled at Mark and walked to the table.

"What's that you've got there, honey?"

Gen glanced at Mark and then her mum.

"Found it in the barn, Mum. Among granddad's tools. Trying to make out what kind of nail it is."

For a second, Gen thought she saw recognition flicker in her mum's eyes, but it was gone immediately. Her mum picked up the nail and rolled it around her hands.

"Among granddad's things, you say? Well, he was a collector of odds and bits. Said it was a hobby of his. Maybe he picked this up from an antiquity shop."

Gen was surprised. She could sense her mum was holding something back.

She had recognized the nail, Gen was sure, but it didn't seem to have the same effect on her as it did Gen.

Gen's mother dropped the nail back on the table and left the kitchen.

"I'll be going to Mrs. Alice's, honey. Do you need anything?"

"No, Mum."

"She seems like a nice person," Mark said as soon as Gen's mum was gone.

"She is. She can be a little intense, but I guess that's how mums are."

"Did you get the feeling that she recognized the nail?"

"I know. I sensed that, but did you notice that nothing happened when Mum touched the nail?"

"She could have suppressed the vision."

"Believe me, it's not an experience you can control. It hits you hard, twists at your very soul. There's no way she could hide such a reaction."

"Then why only you?"

"I don't know. I really wish granddad was here. He would have had an explanation."

"Okay, let me get this straight. You have a nail that was used during the cru—"

"It's not my nail," Gen interrupted. "I think it belongs to my granddad."

"You have a nail…that belongs to your grandfather, but only you react to it. Your mother also knows something about the nail but hasn't told you anything."

Gen nodded.

"Then, there is your grandfather who, before he died, hired me to watch over you."

"He specifically referred to me? I thought you said you were hired to watch over the ranch?"

"He tasked me with the job of keeping you safe. He must have known something was wrong, but so far, all I've seen is a small town with small-town issues. Why spend so much to have someone watch over you?"

Gen and Mark looked at each other, and both were lost in their own thoughts.

❖

The sheriff's office was a small room without any partition. The sheriff's desk sat at one corner of the office with his deputy's at the other corner. Behind them was the only jail in Dundurn.

Sheriff Liam Cuttham sat behind his desk and tried not to look too bored. His son sat across from him, playing a game on his phone. Liam couldn't blame him. Nothing happened in Dundurn. Residents didn't even complain about their neighbors. At least that would have given him a reason to get out of the office.

Nothing new happened anyway. Except if you counted Genesis Isherwood's return as something.

And the stranger, Mark Reynolds.

Sheriff Liam had checked on Mark when Theo had mentioned seeing him at Mr. Gourdeau's memorial service.

Mark Reynolds had checked out. He did operate an independent security outfit way out in Vancouver, but what Liam had found strange was why Mark Reynolds had to have been hired in the first place.

What was going on at the 'Triple 7' ranch?

Mr. Gourdeau had always been slightly eccentric, but Liam had attributed that to his personality.

Liam heard Theo swear out loud and sighed internally.

Liam knew Theo was frustrated over his feelings for Genesis, and he had tried to tell him that they weren't as close as Theo thought anymore.

Theo had been very excited when he'd learned that Genesis was coming back, and Liam had hoped the feeling would have been mutual.

He hadn't been surprised, though.

People change, especially when they left Dundurn and headed to a fancy university to learn business management.

Liam was so engrossed in his thoughts that he didn't notice when Little Pete, who wasn't so little anymore, burst into his office looking very excited. Sheriff Liam couldn't help but feel his blood pressure rise.

"Sheriff, you need to see this." Little Pete ran out, and Liam glanced at his son. Liam got to his feet and collected his hat from the coat rack by his table, wondering what could get Pete so worked up.

Sheriff Liam stepped out of his office with his deputy by his side to see three black SUVs heading towards them. The town folk all stood outside their homes or shops as the cars approached.

Sheriff Liam felt a twinge of apprehension crawl up his spine.

The vehicles stopped abruptly by his office, and Liam waved the dust raised by their approach away from his face.

The vehicles all had tinted windows. Liam watched as a man got out of the middle car. He was smartly dressed in a black suit and sunglasses. He looked to be in his mid-to-late forties but carried himself with authority.

The man walked up to Liam and stopped a few feet away. He pulled off his sunglasses and extended his hand to Liam.

"Good afternoon. My name is Stephen Clarke."

Liam shook the offered hand and ushered Stephen into his office.

❖

Gen sat on her bed, reading her granddad's Bible. Mark had gone to his motel room to change and get a few things.

She had flipped through the pages to see if she could understand her grandfather through the verses he underlined.

She found out that the book of John was extensively underlined and had sidenotes. She read the first chapter and his notes.

"… for as many that received Him, He gave the power to become the sons of God. When we believe in the name of God and accept Him, we become sons and have the right and authority that comes with being sons (and daughters, too)."

Gen smiled.

She continued flipping through and got to the book of Revelations. Here, she could barely read the verses, as there were annotations all over the sides.

Genesis frowned as she read some of the footnotes.

She must come to believe that only in God can she overcome.
The red dragon gives power to the anti-Christ.

As Israel was with child and had to flee from the red dragon, so too must I hide her until the time is right.

Who must he hide? Gen wondered.

Was her grandfather talking about the nail? But he wrote 'her,' and the tone made it seem it was a person, not an object.

Gen continued to read his footnotes.

Sheriff Liam offered Stephen Clarke his seat, but the man had preferred to stand. Liam had had no choice but to stand as well.

"What brings you to Dundurn?"

"I am from the Counter-Terrorism Unit CSIS. We happen to believe that a terrorist is hiding in your town." The man flashed a badge at Liam.

"What?" Liam looked at the man.

A terrorist in Dundurn? The average resident didn't even know what the word meant.

"There has to be a mistake." Liam removed his hat from his head and fanned himself.

"Sorry, sheriff, there is no mistake. We are looking for this person."

Liam realized that the man had been holding a file. The man brought out a portrait of a pretty woman in her mid-twenties.

"No way!"

Theo had been silent by his desk, but Genesis Isherwood's portrait had stirred a reaction from him.

"You are wrong, mister."

The man turned cold eyes to Theo, and he flinched.

"You are mistaken, sir. Gen can't be a terrorist," Theo insisted.

Liam sighed. He had seen some weird things in his life. That's why he had chosen to come to the peaceful town of Dundurn.

But Theo was right, even if Theo was talking from an emotional perspective.

"I think your intel is wrong, Mr. Clarke. Here in Dundurn, we can vouch for everyone."

The man smiled. A cold smile that didn't reach his eyes. The man's eyes remained hard and unrelenting.

"They don't always start out as monsters. Genesis Isherwood was radicalized during her first year at university. Along with her cell, she was the leader and was responsible for the bombing of a bus filled with school children late last year in Toronto. You must have heard of the case."

Liam nodded.

It had been all over the news — a smear on Canada's long record of peace and freedom.

Liam looked at Theo. He could see the pain in his son's eyes mixed with disbelief.

"We were able to capture the leader of another cell who confirmed Miss Isherwood was the mastermind behind the bombing. Just as we were about to raid their hideout, she disappeared. We have reasons to believe that she is here, and she is planning another attack soon."

"Yeah, she is here," Liam reluctantly agreed.

"She came for her granddad's memorial service a couple of weeks ago."

"Thank you. I know this must be hard for you, but we need to act fast."

"Okay. I can take you to Genesis's ranch."

The man nodded and turned to leave. He stopped and stared at Theo.

"You can never really know someone. And the real monsters hide in plain sight." The man nodded again and left the office.

Liam placed his hand on Theo's shoulder. "You said it yourself, son. She had changed. She wasn't the sweet little girl you grew up with."

Theo looked at his dad in anguish.

"But it's Gen. She can't be a terrorist. She cried when Mrs. Pepper lost her husband to cancer. She stayed with the Kellers when their son had the flu. She loves people, Dad."

"You heard him, son. People change. Who knows what happened to her when she went to university? Maybe she was brainwashed or something."

Theo shook his head.

"Not Gen."

Liam had hoped for some action in this dull town but nothing like this.

"Maybe you should stick this one out, son."

Theo nodded absently and watched his dad leave the office.

❖

Gen couldn't believe that the time had passed so fast. She had been engrossed in her granddad's writings, especially regarding the book of Revelation.

Her granddad believed a war was coming. A war between light and darkness, good and evil.

Gen didn't know how she felt about that, but the book of Revelation seemed to predict that, too.

Her phone buzzed, and Gen looked at the caller ID and sighed.

"Hello, Theo."

The line was silent, but she could hear Theo breathing on the other end.

"Theo?"

"You need to get out of there now, Gen. They are coming for you."

N

CHAPTER TEN

Gen stared at the phone in her hand.

Who was coming for her?

She had sensed the fear in Theo's voice, but he hadn't picked up her call when she tried calling back.

It wasn't a prank. Theo had been frightened for her.

Gen dialed a number, and Mark picked up after a couple of seconds.

"Something is wrong," she said, getting straight to the point.

"What is it?"

"Theo just called. He said someone is coming after me."

"Pack a small bag and get out of there now. Head to the nearest motel you can get to. I'll meet you there."

"What's going on, Mark?"

"I don't know, but you need to get out of there. And take the nail with you. Do that now."

"Okay, I'll—"

Gen heard the crunch of gravel as cars turned into the 'Triple 7' ranch. She ran to the window and peeped through.

"They are here, Mark. What do I do?" Gen was scared.

"Stall. I'll be there soon. Don't answer the door or call out to anyone. Wait for me."

The line went dead, and Gen tensed as she heard a loud knock on the door.

❖

Mark dropped his phone and pulled out his traveling bag from under the bed. He unzipped it and brought out a Glock 45, two flash grenades, and a steel-tipped folding knife.

He admired Gen for trying to be strong, but he had heard the quiver in her voice.

Was this why the old man had hired him?

Could he have known that people would come for his granddaughter after his death?

Mark shoved his gun into his belt and placed the remaining items into a small pouch.

He hoped he wasn't too late as he rushed out of his room.

Sheriff Liam knocked on the door for the third time and waited for a response.

"Miss Isherwood? This is Sheriff Liam. We would like to talk to you."

"We are wasting precious time," Stephen Clarke growled. "There's been no answer."

He had suggested breaking down the door, but Liam had ignored his input, as he couldn't produce a search warrant.

"She could be getting away as we stand here twiddling our thumbs like grandmothers in a bingo parlor."

Liam frowned. Who spoke like that?

"Look around you, Mr. Clarke. Where can she run that we won't see her? Your men are at the back. She is completely surrounded, that is, if she's inside."

"She is inside."

That was another thing Liam couldn't quite figure out.

How was Clarke so sure that Genesis was still in the house?

Gen tried to remain as still as she could.

She was glad her parents had chosen today to visit the neighboring farm to help them with a foal that had trouble walking.

She heard the knock on the door and flinched.

Why was Sheriff Liam here? And why had Theo warned her to run?

She would have opened the door if not for Theo's warning. She didn't think she had ever heard him sound so scared.

What was going on?

Mark watched the 'Triple 7' ranch through his binoculars.

He was lying by the road some meters away from the ranch, hidden by a clump of bushes.

He saw Sheriff Liam and a man standing by the door to the house. There were four vehicles in the compound — Liam's van and three black SUVs Mark assumed belonged to whomever was after Gen.

The fact that they were at her doorstep with the sheriff meant they were the real deal or were impersonating law enforcement. Mark couldn't tell which, but he noted how the men surrounding the house carried their weapons. They had training.

Mark looked at the sky. It was getting dark, and that would present the perfect opportunity to get Gen out of there.

Suddenly, Mark watched as big banks of dark clouds gathered and the evening sky grew darker.

He looked at the sky with a puzzled expression.

Where did that come from?

Not wanting to waste the opportunity given, Mark raced towards the ranch as the day turned to night.

Liam looked at the sky in bafflement. The dark cloud had come out of nowhere, and the area had become dark far too quickly to be natural.

He saw Stephen Clarke grit his teeth in annoyance and turn to him. "We enter now!"

"Look here, this is my town, and I say when..."

Something stirred in Stephen Clarke's eyes, and Liam felt terror like never before, even when he had gone to war in Afghanistan.

Clarke's visage seemed to change, and he looked at Liam in disdain.

Two red orbs filled Liam's vision before he realized he was staring into Clarke's eyes.

Hatred marred Clarke's face, and he gripped Liam by the throat.

"I could crush you like the maggot you are, little man, but be thankful I have more pressing matters."

Clarke flung Liam away, and the sheriff sailed through the air. The last thing he heard before he passed out was Clarke muttering under his breath, "The charlatan is here."

Mark cut across the field behind the barn at a steady pace. The night was pitch black, but he wasn't worried. He had surveyed the area countless times over the last couple of weeks, and he had on his night-vision goggles.

68

He saw a guard standing by the barn and slowed his pace. He stilled his heart to reduce the thumping in his chest as he advanced towards the guard.

Mark grabbed the guard from behind and applied pressure to his neck until the guard passed out. He dragged the body away from the barn and quickly searched the body. He found nothing of value and continued his approach.

Gen had said that she was in her bedroom, and from previous reconnaissance, he knew the bedroom was upstairs on the right.

Mark came close to the house and stopped. The area was more heavily guarded, and he counted six guards patrolling the area. There were more in front of the house.

Mark needed a distraction. Some commotion to drive the attention of—

There was an explosion from the front of the house, and he stumbled for a second.

It sounded like the plastic explosives, C4, had gone off.

The guards turned in the direction of the explosion, and Mark dashed forward.

He quickly passed the guards and scaled the tree by the house — a tree with a large branch close to Gen's bedroom window.

He just hoped he wasn't too late.

Gen heard the sound of an explosion from downstairs.

The house shook, and Gen realized that what was after her was far more powerful than she was. She turned to her door when she heard her window slide open.

With a sigh of relief, Gen saw Mark climb into her bedroom.

She hadn't realized she had crossed the room until she was in his arms.

"Are you okay?" Mark asked.

Gen nodded.

"What was that explosion?" he asked.

"I thought that was something that you would know about," Gen replied.

Mark shook his head and placed Gen behind him. He pulled out his Glock 45 and headed out of Gen's bedroom.

Gen followed closely behind Mark, and when they reached the top of the staircase, Mark put his fingers to his lips.

Gen wondered why he stopped when she heard voices coming from downstairs.

❖

Clarke shattered the front door in anger and walked into the house.

The nail was close; he could sense it.

He turned towards the staircase when he heard footsteps coming from the kitchen.

A man walked out of the shadows, and Clarke looked at him in hatred. The man was elderly and had greying hair and visible smiling lines at the sides of his eyes.

"I knew you'd show up sooner or later. You tend to meddle in my business, Myrddin," Clarke said.

"Ah, Atticus, you know as long as I have breath, you can never wield it."

"That can be remedied, Myrddin. You have grown weak over the centuries, while I have increased in the mastery of the arts."

Myrddin watched as Atticus whispered some arcane words, and the air around him rose rapidly in temperature.

A small spherical ball of fire formed in Atticus's hand, and he flung the fireball at Myrddin.

Myrddin felt the ball hurling towards him and stretched out his hand. He grabbed the ball of fire and clenched his fist, snuffing out the fire.

"You really haven't learned anything, Atticus."

Myrddin slapped his palms together, and a blast of wind spread out around him. The wind slammed into Atticus and knocked him out of the shattered front door.

"We don't have much time, Gen," Myrddin called out. "We should hurry."

❖

Gen heard the voices and frowned.

One sounded so familiar, but she couldn't believe her ears.

She walked to the staircase as Mark took her hand. He shook his head as he released her hand and indicated for her to remain behind him.

Gen allowed Mark to lead the way, and they slowly crept down the stairs.

The voices became more precise, and Gen listened.

70

"…over the centuries, while I have increased in the mastery of the arts."

Gen felt the air around her go warm, and there was a whooshing sound.

A blast of wind followed soon after, and she saw a figure hurled out of the front door.

"We don't have much time, Gen. We should hurry."

The words pierced into her soul and seemed to grip her heart in a vice.

Only one person called her in that tone — soft, gentle, and authoritative at the same time.

Gen ran down the stairs before Mark could stop her, and she looked into the smiling face of her granddad.

CHAPTER ELEVEN

"Granddad?"

It couldn't be. Gen had mourned him. Held a memorial service for him.

Yet he stood a few paces from her, a smile tugging the corners of his lips.

Gen raced into her granddad's open arms and hugged him as tight as she could.

"It's all right, Gen," her granddad whispered into her hair. "It's okay."

"Sorry to break this happy reunion, Mr. Gourdeau, but we have company." Mark walked down the stairs and aimed his Glock 45 at the entrance.

Two guards rushed in with semi-automatics, and Mark pulled the trigger. The guards grunted and slumped to the floor, but they were quickly replaced with another two, who entered with their guns blazing.

Mark retreated behind a wall as bullets ricocheted around him.

They would be trapped soon if they didn't get out of the house.

"This way." Gen's granddad grasped Gen's hand and led her towards the kitchen. Mark provided cover and aimed at the two guards, who were smart enough to duck behind walls.

They ran into the kitchen and bolted the door.

"We have to get out of the house, or we'll be trapped," Mark said as he changed the gun's magazine.

Gen's granddad nodded in agreement.

"What do you propose?" he asked.

Mark had a thousand questions he wanted to ask, but he knew now wasn't the time. They needed to get out quickly.

The enemy would be surrounding the house, and the only way out would be to do the unthinkable.

"We go through the front door. It's closer to their cars, and they won't be expecting that."

"Won't there be more of them out front?" Gen asked.

"Most likely, but it's our only way. They are expecting us to come out through the back. The front gives us an element of surprise."

Mark looked towards Gen's granddad. They needed to make a decision quickly.

"It's your show." That was all he said and gave a quirky smile.

Mark shook his head and took a deep breath, clearing his mind of everything.

He needed to be quick, focused, and precise — their lives were in his hands.

Mark opened the door and moved.

His trigger arm extended slightly, with his left hand balancing the weight. Mark swept his arm left and right.

A head peeped out, and Mark pulled the trigger. There was a shout of pain as he advanced, Gen and her granddad following behind.

They needed to be swift. The guards at the back would have heard the noise and know their intention.

He got close to the door when he heard a noise to his right. An intake of breath, a slight movement that would otherwise have gone unnoticed, was loud in his focused state.

Mark swept his left hand out, knocking the semi-automatic away from his side.

There was a rattling sound as the guard pulled the trigger, and plaster from the ceiling fell on them, but Mark was looking at the front door.

A guard rushed in, and Mark pulled the trigger, taking the guard in the chest and knocking him over.

In one fluid motion, Mark swung the butt of his gun across the temple of the guard by his side. The guard grunted and fell.

Mark moved quickly through the front door.

This very moment was crucial. It would be the moment of truth.

If the front door was surrounded, they were dead.

Gen grabbed hold of her granddad's hand and ran after Mark.

Her mind was in turmoil. She still couldn't believe her granddad was alive, and she was holding his hand.

Mark moved like a storm through the room, blowing their enemies away like chaff before a high wind.

She had suspected he was dangerous, but the grace with which he moved stunned her.

They were close to the front door when her granddad shouted at Mark. "Remove your goggles."

Out of instinct or reflex, Mark pulled off his night goggles with his left hand as he swept the area around the front door with his gun.

Gen could hear footsteps, and Mark's gun went off. Somebody stumbled, but the footsteps only increased.

"Both of you, close your eyes," her granddad commanded, and Gen obeyed.

Gen's granddad raised his hand into the air, and the night flared brightly for a couple of seconds.

There were shouts of surprise as the guards running towards them stumbled and fell.

Gen opened her eyes and saw Mark run towards one of the SUVs, and she and her granddad followed.

"You never cease with the parlor tricks, Myrddin," a voice said behind them, and Gen spun around.

Atticus dusted his suit off as he strode towards them.

Mark heard the voice and reacted instantly. He recognized the voice as the one that had spoken with Gen's granddad in the house.

Myrddin.

Why was he calling Gen's granddad by that name? the thought came fleetingly to Mark's mind as he aimed his gun at the stranger and pulled the trigger.

Mark watched in amazement as the man flicked his hand, and he heard a ping sound as the bullet penetrated the metal of the SUV parked close by.

Impossible!

Mark knew he hadn't missed. Not this close.

He aimed again and pulled the trigger repeatedly, but all he heard was the pinging sound as bullets seemed to be diverted away from the man.

Myrddin watched as Atticus walked towards them after deflecting the bullets from Mark's gun away from himself.

"Gen, get behind me," her granddad instructed. Gen obeyed and watched as Atticus stopped some meters from them.

"All I want is what she carries, Myrddin. Give me that, and they get to live."

"Why must we go about this dance, Atticus? Why would I give you the nail?"

"She is ignorant of its use, Myrddin. I have no fear of her."

Gen's granddad laughed.

"Then you don't know my granddaughter, Atticus. She will learn, and she will be your demise. I have seen it, and it will surely come to pass."

"Then we must make sure her corpse will be all that remains here."

Atticus stretched out his hand, and lightning edged out of his fingers towards Gen.

At the same time, Myrddin formed a circle in the air, and the lightning slammed into a barrier.

Mark read the situation in an instant.

He was outmatched, and he could do nothing.

A part of his mind rebelled at the fact that he saw lightning shoot out of the stranger's fingers.

Lightning!

He saw Gen's granddad somehow summon a barrier that stopped the lightning.

The fight seemed to go back and forth, with arcs of lightning targeting them and a wall stopping them.

Mark quickly reassessed the situation.

They had a joker on their side who somehow could level the playing field.

If Gen's grandad and Atticus were evenly matched, maybe he could tip the scale in their favor.

Mark watched and waited, and when the time was right, he acted.

Gen's granddad wasn't only on the defensive, but he also shot out focused bolts of strong air at Atticus.

Mark waited for such an attack and drew out his military blade. He swung the knife at Atticus, who sent a lightning bolt to snap the blade in half.

Gen's granddad saw the opening created by Atticus's distraction and acted.

He sent a bolt of air that slammed into Atticus and sent him sailing across the ranch.

"Now would be a good time to make our getaway before he comes back," Gen's granddad said.

Mark didn't need to be told again. He leaped into the SUV they had been running to and started the vehicle. Gen and her granddad rushed in, and he raced out of the ranch.

"Just what the heck happened back there? Who were they?" Mark demanded as he sped off.

"And why was that man calling you Myrddin, Granddad?"

"That's my name, Gen."

"So, who were they? Better still, how are you alive?" Mark asked.

Gen looked at her granddad and waited for an answer. As much as she loved that he was here with her, everybody believed that he was dead.

"It's pretty obvious I'm not dead, isn't it?"

"Then why the act? Why go through all that?"

"It's a bit complicated, Gen. Events have been set in motion that shape the course of humanity. It was expedient that the ruse is done—"

"I don't understand a word you just said, Mr. Gourdeau. If that is really your name."

"It's my name."

"Be plain, Granddad. What is going on? Who was that man, and why did you feel that you had to lie to everybody...including me?"

The SUV swerved as Mark avoided a pothole. He looked in the rear mirror to make sure they weren't being followed.

"I regret having to do that to you, Gen, but it was the only way."

"The only way for what?"

"The only way to get you to come back home."

"But all you had to do was call me to come home. You know I would have listened to you, Granddad."

"Would you?" Myrddin asked softly. "I needed you to come back not only to the ranch but also in here." Myrddin gently tapped Gen in the chest.

"You are more important than you realize, Gen."

"Because of the nail?" Gen instinctively touched the pocket of her jeans. Walking had been awkward and uncomfortable, the nail stabbing her thigh.

"Among other things."

"What other things?"

"You will get to know soon, Gen."

"So, who was that guy?" Mark asked.

"Atticus?"

"Yeah. And is this Atticus the real deal? Was that magic I saw back there? Do you do magic, too?" Mark needed to know what and who he was up against so that he could plan adequately.

"Atticus has been after the nail for a while now. We are lucky that he was the only one that came."

"I don't feel lucky. And are you saying there are more of them that can fling magic around?"

"That estimation would be truly correct," Myrddin answered.

"So, let me get this straight. This Atticus is after the nail used to crucify Jesus Christ." Mark saw Myrddin raise an eyebrow in the rearview mirror. "Your granddaughter told me."

Myrddin looked at Gen.

"I had a vision when I touched the nail, Granddad."

"Wait, the nail was protected by a…for want of a better word… a spell. This was done to prevent it from being detected. A potent spell, I must add. And you were able to touch it?"

Gen didn't know if she should be proud that she broke her granddad's spell or worried.

And her granddad could cast spells?

"Can you explain everything from the beginning, Granddad?" Gen asked.

"That would take some telling, but what I can say for now is that Atticus and his fellows want the nail to end their existence."

"They need the nail to kill themselves? Just what are they?" Mark asked.

"They have been around for millennia, cursed to wander the earth. Now the nail has the intent or, in this case, the power since it has pierced the flesh of the living Son of God. They believe that power can destroy the curse on them."

"And can it?" Gen wondered.

"Yes, it can."

"Then why are we keeping it away from them? They don't look like happy-go-lucky kind of guys. Won't we be doing humanity justice by getting rid of them?" Mark couldn't understand.

"That would have been great, but that approach is exactly what our enemy wants. If we destroy them, then the nail and the inherent power will also be destroyed. And I can assure you, the nail is still very much needed because Atticus and his fellow deviants aren't the real problems."

Mark continued speeding down the highway, unsure of his destination, and the car was silent as Gen and Mark digested that piece of information.

Mark sensed the wariness in Myrddin's voice.

What could be more dangerous than Atticus? he wondered.

"The real problem is the red dragon," Gen whispered.

Myrddin looked at Gen in appreciation.

"I have been reading your Bible, Granddad. I saw the note you left for me."

"Now, who or what is the red dragon?" Mark sounded lost.

If he hadn't seen what he saw back at the ranch, Mark would have called Gen and her granddad two crazy people he had had the misfortune of meeting.

"The red dragon must be afraid of the nail," Gen continued. "So, it fits into his plans if this Atticus finds the nail and destroys it."

"But more than that, Gen, he fears the keeper of the nail, for he understands what prophecy has said. And one prophesy states that the woman shall wax strong because of knowledge and shall overturn his plans and cut short his operations. "That is what the nail brings more than anything," Myrddin said.

"Knowledge? Knowledge of what?"

"Even I have only been its guardian, Gen. That I cannot answer. For I know only in part."

Mark looked at Myrddin in the rearview mirror and wondered, *Just who the heck are you?*

CHAPTER TWELVE

Mark ditched the SUV at the first filling station they got to, and they hitched a ride to Saskatoon. Mark paid cash at a car rental, and they drove to his motel room.

"We need to be on the move, so I suggest we head to Vancouver or, better still, out of the country," Mark suggested.

"I'm not leaving my parents."

"We can make arrangements for them..."

Gen shook her head. "I think for now, we remain near Dundurn as much as possible."

"Why?" Mark was curious. It didn't make sense to remain when there was the opportunity of retreating or fleeing.

"Let's just say it's better for everything if we are here," Myrddin voiced out.

"Okay, so, what's the plan? We do have one, don't we?

"Of course, we do. The original plan was to lie low and learn, but things went a little sideways with that one."

"So, presently, we don't have one," Mark noted.

He looked at Myrddin and then Gen.

Okay, it's not too bad, he said to himself.

"Can they be killed without the nail?"

"Atticus? Not that I know of."

"Is this the only nail we have?"

"Presently, yes."

"How many are like Atticus?"

"There are three others."

Gen's mind flashed to the vision she had experienced — four Roman soldiers were fighting over a robe.

"They are four," she stated. "They fought over Jesus's clothes. One of them is called Luc...eh...Lucilius!" Gen snapped her finger in remembrance.

She saw Myrddin looking at her.

"Lucilius is the leader, and you are right. They scourged Jesus and battered the Messiah's belongings and were cursed. They have long wandered the earth, and they have a craving for holy artifacts. They have amassed quite a collection."

"Hold up. Atticus was alive during the time of Jesus Christ?" Mark was amazed.

"Not only were they all alive then, but they also partook in his crucifixion. They beat him and mocked him and took delight in his suffering."

Myrddin's words hung in the air as Gen remembered the anguish and pain she had seen Jesus suffer in her vision.

"And they know you," Mark stated. It wasn't a question, as he remembered Myrddin and Atticus's conversation.

"Yes, we have crossed paths numerous times."

Mark frowned.

Why did Gen's granddad's name sound familiar?

"And he called you Myrddin," Gen added.

Myrddin looked at Gen with a smile on his face, waiting for her to make the connections.

"Who are you?" Mark whispered.

"I am Myrddin Emrys Wylit."

Mark felt power surround Myrddin as he boldly proclaimed his name. The sense of power finally snapped the puzzle into place for Mark.

Mark had loved fairy tales as a kid. Tales of King Arthur and the Knights of the Round Table. He had imagined himself being Lancelot at one time, but he had grown up.

Fairy tales weren't real. They were…fairy tales.

"You are the Merlin," Mark said in wonder.

Gen looked at her granddad and saw that he didn't refute Mark's statement.

Could it be true? Was she standing before an iconic figure? If so…

"Then, you're not really my granddad?"

Myrddin looked at Gen and placed his hand on her shoulder. "Maybe not by blood, but by something just as strong. I have been by your family's side for generations, both as a guardian and protector. I have watched you grow into the fine woman you are today, and I'll always be proud to be your granddad."

Gen wiped tears from her eyes.

"So, how old are you?" she asked with a laugh.

"I am quite old, Gen."

"And how did you get involved in all of this?" Mark asked.

"I had an encounter, young man. It changed my life, and I saw the darkness rising on the earth. For years, I pondered the meaning of my vision until I was led to Jerusalem. I met one of your ancestors Gen, Empress Helena, and mother to Constantine the Great. She was in my vision, and she was led to discover the burial place of the true cross and nails."

"Nails? There are more?" Mark asked.

"There were three nails that were used to crucify the Messiah. Helena gave two to her son, who rose to be a great emperor, for she thought he would be the one to fight the darkness."

"And the last nail?"

"The foot nail. The most potent of the three nails, for it is believed to have absorbed some of the soul's essence. History believes that Empress Helena sensed that if it fell into the wrong hands, it would bring about the apocalypse, so she threw it into the Baltic Sea. History, as you can see, was wrong, for in your hands, my dear, lies the foot nail of the cross."

Silence reigned in the tiny motel room as the gravity of the situation hit them.

"What am I meant to do with it?" Gen's voice trembled. She was weighed down by the responsibility she had to bear.

"You will know when the time is right, my warrior princess."

Gen tried to smile but couldn't shake the feeling that she would fail.

Theo looked around the 'Triple 7' ranch. The place looked like a war zone.

There was a big hole where the front door should be.

Theo had tired of waiting at the sheriff's office and had decided to check the ranch himself.

Theo saw his dad's van and ran to it. He passed the back of the truck and saw his dad's body slumped against the side of the car.

"Dad!" Theo screamed as he ran to his dad's side.

Sheriff Liam stared blankly at nothing, and Theo stretched a shaking hand to feel his dad's neck for a pulse. Theo sighed in relief as he felt a faint beat.

What had happened here? Had he misjudged Gen? Was she really a terrorist?

The front door looked as though an explosion had shattered it to pieces.

He had checked around, but the ranch was empty. There had been empty shell casings around the house, and it was apparent there had been a gunfight.

He had also seen splashes of blood on the ground.

Something terrible had happened here, but all that remained was his dad's broken body as evidence of the violence that had taken place.

Theo picked up his walkie-talkie and clicked it on.

He would get help for his father. Then, Genesis Isherwood had a lot to answer for.

❖

Mark stood watch by the window while Gen slept on the bed. Myrddin sat on the only chair with his hands clasped in his lap and his eyes closed.

He had a meditative pose, but Mark had a feeling he was aware of everything around him.

Mark didn't mind the silence, for it gave him time to think.

His job technically was done. He was hired to protect Gen, but that was because he had believed that her grandfather was dead.

His client wasn't as dead as he had led Mark to believe. Even if his client was the legendary magician Merlin, he could walk away if he wanted to. That was obviously a breach of contract.

And what use was he against magic?

How do you combat a foe that could deflect bullets and snap steel with lightning?

The odds were heavily against him.

So, why did he feel a sense of duty to the young woman sleeping on his bed?

Whatever was expected of her was more significant than him.

What help could he render? Would it be enough?

On the desk lay his weapons. Mark wasn't taking any chances. He had an M4 Carbine, his Glock 45, a flash grenade, and a 'door sweeper,' his homemade miniature C4 explosives.

"I knew your forefather. Met him briefly, but he left a lasting impression."

Mark turned to see Myrddin staring at him.

"What do you mean?"

"I didn't choose you out of chance, Mark Reynolds. You still have a role to play in this fight against the darkness."

"And what role would that be?"

"The same as all your lineage. To keep the keeper safe. To protect my granddaughter. Your forefather was the first to accept that role. He kept Empress Helena alive and fought the accursed to protect her. He was a skilled warrior, as are you. Don't doubt yourself."

Mark stared at Myrddin and wondered how he saw into the hearts of men.

"What ancestor are you talking about? Who was he?"

"He was a respected man who believed in honor and integrity. He was a captain in the Praetorian guard before it was disbanded."

Mark nodded in gratitude. He stood silently by the window and watched Myrddin.

"I thought I would have months to prepare her. Guide her on the right path. I didn't foresee this. Her future and decisions are like flux in the oceán of the prophetic. I had to adjust my plans."

"So, you staged your death intending to draw her back to this town. What were you planning to do afterward?"

"I would reveal myself to her and tell her everything. Guide her as I was meant to all these years. You see, prophesy states that the seventy-seventh generation of the lineage of Empress Helena would be able to wield the instrument of the dragon's destruction."

"And I take it your granddaughter is the seventy-seventh descendant."

"Yes. But what I'd failed to project was the influence of the enemy. When she was accepted to university, the enemy saw an opportunity to thwart God's plan. I saw her slipping away."

"So, you adjusted your plans too. Faked your death to lure her back home. If that was your intention, why didn't you reveal yourself to her sooner?"

"Again, the future turned in the direction I didn't expect, for something unforeseen happened."

Mark looked at Myrddin when he paused, clearly pondering what he would say next.

"I sensed the presence of the second nail."

"The second of the three nails that were used to crucify Christ?"

Myrddin nodded.

"While the other two nails aren't as potent as the foot nail, they still contain power in their own right. I went to investigate the surge of power I had felt, and I left you in place to protect her. She wasn't meant to find the foot nail so soon. Lucilius and Atticus sensed the foot nail and hoped to retrieve it for themselves."

"So, did you get the second nail?" Mark asked.

"No, but I know where it is. One of the accursed has it in his possession."

Mark took the revelation without batting an eye. Somehow, he wasn't surprised that their enemy had one of the nails.

"If one of the four has it, why hasn't he used it?"

"I don't know, but I can guess. The nails are drawn to each other. Maybe they want to get their hands on both nails."

"The nails sense each other! And you're just mentioning that fact now. We have to get out of here."

"Relax, Mark Reynolds. They cannot find us so soon."

Mark tried to relax but couldn't. He imagined facing Atticus again and shuddered. He would be dead if Myrddin hadn't shown up when he did.

How do you face an enemy as strong as that?

"If the nails can sense each other, can we sense the nail with them?"

"I believe so. But for me to do that, I'd need to prepare myself mentally."

Mark grunted. He hadn't been thinking of Myrddin when he asked the question.

"What of someone who has already bonded with the foot nail?

Myrddin turned to Gen's sleeping form.

"What do you have in mind?"

"Oh, just thinking of paying them back in their own coin. If we can sense the accursed, we can set a trap for them and hopefully get the second nail."

"A bold move."

"And it has the element of surprise. But for it to work, there is an element of risk," Mark stated.

"We have to leave Gen unguarded while we make our attack."

Mark nodded.

If they took Gen with them, their enemy would sense the nail and know they were coming. The only way the plan stood a chance of working would be to leave Gen with the nail.

Gen stirred in the bed, mumbling in her sleep, and Mark and Myrddin paused the conversation to watch her. Gen's mumbling stopped, and they resumed their discussion.

"I like your plan, but you will stay with Gen. She cannot remain unprotected, even for a moment."

Mark had been expecting that. He had nothing to offer in terms of fighting power, so he would probably be a liability if he went along with Myrddin.

"Fair enough. When do we start?"

"No time like the present, I'm told."

"Okay, we give her a couple of hours to rest, then we make our move."

Myrddin smiled at Mark. "As I said, you are needed more than you think."

Mark accepted the compliment with a nod of his head. He looked at Myrddin in the ensuing silence.

"Can I ask you a question?" Mark asked.

Myrddin looked up and opened his arms wide, and Mark took that as consent.

"Why here?" Mark saw the look of confusion on Myrddin's face. "What I mean is why this place? This town? You could have gone anywhere. Why choose here?"

Myrddin turned and looked away, and Mark thought he wouldn't answer the question.

"I kept losing them," Myrddin said pensively. "I couldn't save them all. Anywhere we went, the accursed found us quickly. The accursed seemed to have a network of soldiers and resources that made finding us easy. I had a duty to Empress Helena's lineage, and I was failing woefully. The longest we stayed in one place was six months, and we had to move or risk discovery. We eventually found a place in France, and for a while, things seemed peaceful. I suppose I got careless. I had set up the basic concealment spell over the foot nail, and I assumed that would be enough. Marie was a very inquisitive girl, and like Gen, she found the nail sooner than I had expected. I came home one evening after scouting the region to find Marie and her family dead. The accursed had been systematic, ensuring no one survived their invasion. They had taken the foot nail, and I had to confront them to get it back. Luckily, it was Remus that came for the nail, the weakest of them. I got the nail back, but I thought the mission was over. I thought I had failed."

Myrddin sighed as he remembered past pains and sorrows. Mark felt bad for bringing the issue up and remained silent, waiting for Myrddin to resume talking. The silence stretched as Myrddin seemed lost in a past event.

Mark moved from the window and sat on the edge of the bed, careful not to disturb Gen.

"What happened, Myrddin?"

"What?"

"What happened? They all died, so how is Gen a descendant?"

Myrddin smiled ruefully. "I wandered the countryside for days, confused and thinking about my next step. I prayed and listened, waiting for instructions. The answer came most strangely. I was in a pub one evening when a conversation came up, a conversation about the gruesome murder of Marie and her family. Some of the people wondered how the dastardly act of evil men could erase a bloodline. It was there that a barmaid — I can still remember her face — shocked people by whispering that Marie's father had a bastard child. She was timid, you see, and had barely spoken above a whisper, but everyone in the pub had heard."

"I met up with her afterward and found the name of a woman living not too far from the pub. A woman with a young girl named Helena. How ironic could that be? It was as though God had painted an arrow over the child's head, saying, 'This is the one.'"

"I realized something at that moment. No one knew about the child because she had been in a remote area. I took that as a sign and decided to adjust my plans accordingly. There had been rumors of explorers venturing into the wild and going as far as across the Atlantic. What better place to hide the jewel so priceless than where no one would know what gems are? I convinced the mother, and we boarded a ship for North America. The rest, as they say, is history."

Mark nodded again and felt the need to say something, but the comfortable silence that followed seemed to speak enough for Mark.

Theo sat in the back of the ambulance with his father strapped to the gurney. The EMTs had arrived at the 'Triple 7' ranch as quickly as they could. Theo had sat by his father; a finger pressed on Liam's throat to be sure that he was still alive. The EMT had said he was in a coma and didn't know if he'd make the trip to the general hospital in Saskatoon.

Theo listened to the sound of the siren as the ambulance sped along the road.

Gen had caused this. Directly or indirectly, she was to blame.

Theo remembered her whispered conversation with the stranger in the barn when Theo had decided to check on Gen to make sure she was safe.

Had they been plotting an attack right under his nose? Theo felt disgusted with himself. He had thought Gen was still the sweet innocent girl he had known growing up. How could he be so wrong?

And he had helped her escape.

Everything had been peaceful before she came back to Dundurn.

She had brought pain and suffering with her. Everyone knew her granddad had died from a broken heart because Gen had abandoned her family when she went to university and had suddenly become too good for the townsfolk of Dundurn.

She had caused this, Gen, and the stranger. They had destroyed his life.

Now his father was struggling for his life.

Theo gritted his teeth.

She would pay for the suffering she had caused and for the pain that she had spread around.

She would pay.

The ambulance sped along the highway, heading for Saskatoon.

N

CHAPTER THIRTEEN

Gen woke, and Mark told her about their plan. She agreed to help but looked first to Myrddin for a response.

"How do I even do that? All I get when I touch the nail are visions."

"I can't tell you much, Gen, but Empress Helena also started off by getting visions. As time grew, she began to know things. She saw the past, the present, and the future. Glimpses that guided us and taught us how to plan for today." Myrddin paused. "She once saved our lives because she could sense the other nail and the evil that were the accursed."

Gen sighed. While that was helpful information, it still didn't tell her how Empress Helena could sense the other nail.

"I think you need to focus, Gen. Maybe…think of the other nail. Think of it as trying to reach out to someone, like making a phone call."

Gen nodded and tried to relax. Her heart had sped up from realizing the task she had been assigned. She took a deep breath to calm herself and brought out the nail from her pocket. She placed the handkerchief on the bed and unfolded it.

The nail sat in the middle of the handkerchief, and Gen concentrated on it. She was wary of going back to the cross at Golgotha.

Focus on the other nail, Gen chided herself.

Taking another breath, Gen reached out and grabbed the nail.

She was transported immediately.

Gen looked around in trepidation. She wasn't at Golgotha but somewhere else. There was a large crowd in front of her, and Gen walked towards it.

People sat around a little hilltop and listened to a man who sat at the top of the hill. His words flowed down to the people amassed around him.

Gen felt drawn to the man on the hilltop. As he drew closer to the end of the crowd, his voice echoed down to her.

"…you are the salt of the earth, but if the salt loses its taste, of what use is it? It is now good for nothing…"

Gen listened in amazement. The man spoke Aramaic, and she could understand him.

"...you are the light of the world. A city that is upon a hill cannot stay hidden. Nobody lights a candle and puts it under a bowl. But it is placed on a stand so that everyone in the house can see the candlelight. Likewise, let your light shine before everybody so that they may see your good deeds and give our heavenly Father the glory."

Gen knew without a doubt that she sat before Jesus Christ. She couldn't make out His appearance, as she was far from where He was, but His words resonated with power.

We are the light of the world. We give light to a world in darkness.

Gen pondered on this as the world warped around her, and she found herself in a garden that was scattered with clusters of olive trees. And, between these groups of olive trees, some pathways connected them.

Gen strolled along the pathways, trying to get her bearing.

It was night, but she knew she was still in her vision. The same alienness of her surroundings filled her heart.

Was she in Jerusalem?

Gradually, she began to pick up on a muted sound.

She wasn't alone. Stilling her beating heart, Gen tried to pinpoint the source of the sound. She had always been a spectator in these visions, so she didn't think she could be hurt.

Or could she?

Fear clouded her mind. Her granddad hadn't mentioned anything like that. All of this was new to her.

The sound grew louder, and she followed it to the source, trusting her hearing.

She saw a group of people huddled together to stave off the biting cold beneath an olive tree. They were all asleep, and she could hear the faint sound of snoring.

This wasn't what had caught her attention, though. The noise had been more of a groan — a deep desire to bear off a heavy load.

Gen moved on.

She found the source of the groaning some meters from the sleeping group.

A man knelt by a small stone. The air around him carried a heavy burden that pressed against Gen's soul.

She couldn't go any further. The pressure dropped her to her knees, and she found herself groaning in despair, too.

The load, the pressure of whatever was in the air, was becoming unbearable. It seemed like the weight of the world pressed down on her spirit, and her heart felt ready to shatter.

Gen tried to crawl back but could only feel her body crushing against the hard earth.

She could still see the man who she now knew was in the throes of combat.

Not combat of physical hands but one of the spirits, for she felt a slight touch of the pressure the man was under.

"Father, I know you can do all things. I would be glad if this cup will pass from me, but I remain humble to your will and not my own," the man said.

He must be Jesus, Gen thought.

This was the anguish he felt as he knew he would be betrayed by Judas and crucified.

Just when Gen felt her soul would shatter from the spiritual pressure, she blinked.

Gen gasped and tried to take a gulping breath. Her heart felt like it would explode. She saw Mark and her granddad rush to her side, and she quickly shook her head.

The pressure was gone, but she still felt traces of the stress she had experienced as if she had lost a limb.

"What's wrong?" Mark asked, confused and worried.

"He suffered so much," she blurted as her gaze searched for something. Something that was not there. They looked at her in confusion.

"I saw him, Granddad...I saw Jesus! I...I felt a little of his anguish." Her body trembled as the words left her mouth.

How could a single being survive that?

Eventually, coming back to reality, Gen saw the concerned looks on Myrddin and Mark's faces.

"I'll be all right. Just need a moment," she reassured them.

"Were you able to sense anything?" Mark asked after a moment.

Gen shook her head in response.

"I don't know what happened. It's like the visions wanted me to see these sights. I had no control."

"It's okay. Helena had these periods where she seemed sucked in by the visions. She told me maybe God was trying to get her attention."

Gen tried to smile.

"What do we do now?"

"You rest. We'll try again later."

Gen nodded again. She suddenly felt an overwhelming desire to lie down and close her eyes. Within seconds, she was dozing.

Mark looked at Gen's sleeping form and turned to Myrddin.

"This is your doing?" he asked.

"She needed the rest. The vision had taken a lot from her. I fear she's going too fast. Her predecessor only got to this stage after months of teachings and studying the word of God."

Mark continued to look at Gen, concerned.

"Can she do it?"

"I believe that she can. She's at a crossroads in her life. The influence of the enemy still lingers, and she needs to purge it out."

"How does she do that?" A fight he could not entirely comprehend. There were rules and strategies to employ.

"We must all walk our individual paths, Mark Reynolds."

"And was this your path, Myrddin Emrys Wylit?" Mark questioned. Myrddin grimaced, scratching his chin.

"I've done things I'm not proud of, but I had my own Damascus experience. I was once a druid in the service of my people. There were lines I crossed because I felt the end justified the means. We were at war with the Irish for our land, and I was tasked with leading our people. One night, I had a vision of a man in bright and shining light. He showed me the real enemy that night. A darkness so vast and oppressive. The man's shining light pierced through that thick darkness and…the darkness fled."

Myrddin continued, "That man in bright light was Jesus Christ of Nazareth. I yielded my life in His service in fighting the darkness I had seen, and He showed me when the nails would be found. Decades later, I met Empress Helena. The rest is history, as they say."

Mark grunted. He would have disbelieved Myrddin's story, but what he had seen was testament and proof to his words.

"So, who are the accursed? They are the ones after the nail."

"Atticus, you have met. The others go by the names Remus and Lucilius. Lucilius is their leader."

"That's three. I thought Gen said they were four?"

"They were, but Marius was killed."

"So, they can die?" Mark derived.

"Yes, but at great costs. Helena sacrificed her life to kill Marius."

Mark was silent as he thought of losing Gen. He would make sure that that never happened.

"Can they all do magic?"

"No. Atticus is a practitioner of the dark arts. Remus is…for lack of a better word, a shapeshifter."

"A shapeshifter?" Mark raised an eyebrow.

"That's the best I can come up with."

"And the last one?"

"Lucilius is a skilled swordsman. A weapon master."

Mark nodded. Knowing your enemy was the first step to victory. *Beating the crap out of them would be an excellent second step*, Mark thought.

How strong would Lucilius be to control a magician and a shapeshifter?

Mark clenched his fist.

Would he survive if he went one on one with him?

He couldn't help but wonder.

Theo drove the sheriff's van into town. The road was deserted as he went, all Dundurn residents having turned in for the night a while ago. He had stood and stared at the dent made by his father's body on the door of the van.

What could throw his father that hard to bend metal?

His father wasn't a frail old man, and his gun had still been holstered.

Theo turned into the parking space by the sheriff's office when he noticed the same black SUV from earlier in the day parked there.

He got out of his van and slammed the door in anger. He watched as Stephen Clarke got out of the SUV and headed towards him.

"I am very sorry about your father. He was a good man."

"He is alive…but in an induced coma. There is swelling on the brain and a punctured lung. What happened at the 'Triple 7'?"

"I told your father that Genesis Isherwood was a dangerous individual, but he wouldn't listen. He walked to the door to talk with her. The door was rigged with explosives, and the blast caught him. It looked like she was ready for us, as though she knew we were coming."

Stephen Clarke's glare cut into Theo, and Theo looked away guiltily.

He would never forgive himself for trusting Gen. His father was at death's door because of her.

"What do we do now?"

Stephen Clarke shrugged.

"We can only wait and hope that she makes a mistake or reaches out to a family member."

Theo looked up, suddenly remembering that her parents had gone to Johanssen's farm.

"I think we need to get back to the 'Triple 7.' Genesis Isherwood's parents went to a neighbor's farm. Their horse had a little complication which Gen's parents helped with. They've been going there every Thursday to check on the foal."

Clarke looked at Theo and smiled.

"I'll call for backup. We'll impose a lockdown on this town to make sure Genesis Isherwood doesn't escape. Maybe the parents know something. She is their daughter, after all."

Theo frowned as he tried to picture Mr. and Mrs. Isherwood helping a terrorist, even their daughter.

"I don't know about that."

"We'll put a detail to watch the ranch in case Genesis tries to contact her parents."

Theo quickly agreed. The only one that needed to be punished for her crimes was Genesis Isherwood.

CHAPTER FOURTEEN

ROAD TO CONSTANTINOPLE 327 A.D.

The carriage jostled Empress Helena about as the wheels ran over large pebbles and stones. Helena peered through the curtain of the carriage to see the escort of six guards following.

She caught the eye of one of the guards in the lead and smiled. She was glad to see Calisto with her again. Knowing he was close by made her feel safe.

He had demanded he sit with her in the wagon for her safety, but she had refused. The wagon could barely contain her and the two small chests she carried back to Constantinople. Having him in the wagon would have made her claustrophobic. The guards were dressed in simple civilian attire with their weapons wrapped in a blanket against their saddles. Helena had rarely seen Calisto out of uniform, and she had to agree that civilian clothes looked good on him. He had a build that would make even sack-cloth look good on him, not that the young fool noticed such trivialities.

Calisto was a man bred for war. They were riding to Constantinople in disguise.

Merlin had been adamant that her return trip be as unassuming as possible. A carriage with a platoon of soldiers had gone the day before, taking the main route to Constantinople. Merlin had ridden with the carriage, dressed as a nobleman. He hoped to draw the attention of the four away while she took the less scenic route home.

The wagon rattled again, and Helena wondered if her aged bones would remain in one piece by the time she got to the palace. They still had a long way to go, and the leisurely pace did not seem too promising.

Empress Helena had found peace in the few weeks she had stayed in Jerusalem with Merlin. He had told her of his own journey in serving God and the many tribulations and trials he had faced. His experiences had made her sorrow for her grandson seem a fickle thing. While she couldn't deny the pain and hurt in her heart at Crispus's execution by her own son, she had to move on.

God had a plan for her life, and the hurt and pain of Crispus's loss had drowned his will for her life.

Helena realized that the whispers in the night had started when she had mourned for her dead grandson. Thoughts of revenge at the perpetrators of her pain had clouded her mind and heart.

Constantine must have sensed it and asked her to come to Jerusalem to search for the holy relics. Initially, Helena had thought that Constantine only wanted to distract her. Now, she saw the finger of God in his decision to send her forth to Jerusalem.

She had found the nails.

Merlin had been worried that carrying the nails out of the house they had been hiding in would invite trouble, hence, the ruse they had thought of. She had added a straightforward suggestion as an idea had sprung into her heart.

Empress Helena had gone back to the site of her excavation with a regiment of soldiers. The site had been plundered and the crosses gone, but she had seen pieces left.

She had wondered how she could hide the nails in plain sight while still fulfilling her heart's desire of keeping her son alive. Helena looked at the small chests by her feet and smiled.

She knew the nails possessed power, but she hadn't figured they would be this strong, especially the foot nail.

Helena had instructed a forge be erected, and an exceptionally gifted blacksmith had hammered a shape out of the nails as he muttered something — a spell, perhaps — under his breath. It was a simple reshaping that had made the two objects more conveniently portable.

In one chest was a bridle. One nail had been fashioned into simple rings to connect the parts of the harness together. It was inconspicuous and wouldn't merit a second glance.

In the second chest, there was a helmet — a plain helmet made of iron and gold. But Merlin had used a spell to forge the second nail into the two clamps that fastened the helmet to the head.

Apart from hiding the nails in plain sight, Helena's agents had brought word of unrest among the capital's political council. She needed her son to stay safe.

Emperor Constantine had made many positive changes for Christians in the empire. She was sure that others were unhappy with his policies, but Helena believed the power of the nails would keep him safe and drive away evil. She had seen firsthand the nails' strength in the cavern when she had struck that assassin.

She hid the last nail close to her body. The foot nail was wrapped in a thin strip of cloth and tied to her inner thigh.

❖

Calisto looked around the wagon warily. He had been apprehensive ever since the journey began and didn't think he would relax until it was over.

Upon separating from his two guards, he had located the Barking Inn — a broken and down-on-its-luck tavern where people met. The bar wasn't known for its excellent meals and drinks and stood empty all year round. Still, Calisto had formed an agreement with the tavern owner. The man was an agent working for him. Calisto had approached him during one of Empress Helena's visits to Jerusalem. Seeing the frequency with which she visited Palestine and the surrounding cities, Calisto deemed it necessary to have a foothold in the town's status and news.

The tavern owner, a short, brutish man in his mid-fifties, had a network of beggars and ruffians. While not the most pleasing profession, they were everywhere and were hardly noticed by the people who passed them and moved on with their lives.

One such beggar had brought word that a woman fitting Empress Helena's description had been seen a couple of streets down in a derelict part of town.

Calisto had gone to the location and waited by the house. He had borrowed the beggar's worn and torn clothes to blend in. The elderly man that had vanished with Empress Helena had walked up to him and asked him to follow.

Calisto had been surprised. He had imagined that his disguise would pass scrutiny, but the fellow had seen through his attempt at deception.

"How did you know it was me?" Calisto had demanded. The man had smiled with eyes that seemed to pierce through Calisto's soul.

"Your light cannot be hidden, young man. I saw you a mile away and wanted to spare you the discomfort of sleeping by the roadside."

Calisto had shaken his head at the man's reply.

"Is she safe?"

"She is…for now. But know this, the four of them will never stop searching for what she holds."

"The four?"

"The four accursed. The scourge of the earth and the epitome of despair and pain."

The man had looked at Calisto and intoned in a deep voice.

"Beware of the wormwood and the speaker of lies. Stand fast and stand sure, for the safety of a million rests in your hands." The man looked confused for a second before he cleared his throat.

"Take heed of what you just heard, boy. Danger will come when you least expect it."

Calisto had followed the man, and even though Calisto hadn't understood the man's words, the words had imprinted on his soul.

Beware of the wormwood and the speaker of lies.

Calisto looked around again, with the words of the man who he later knew to be Merlin, resounding in his heart.

The path looked peaceful, and the heat was not oppressive— at least not as much as usual. The driver of the wagon hummed a gentle tune as the two horses plodded along. Calisto looked back and spotted the occasional shrub or plant.

The journey looked peaceful, but Calisto expected trouble. Merlin's words rang louder in his soul the farther they went.

Calisto also sighed in relief when the horses neighed, and the driver pulled to a stop. He was bred for action, and this he could understand.

Calisto and the guards flicked the reins on their horses and moved forward. Calisto immediately noticed a lone rider waiting in the middle of the road some meters ahead of them.

It seemed that they enjoyed attacking individually. The man looked plain, but Calisto knew that looks could be deceptive. Instead, Calisto watched for other telltale signs.

The man sat upright on the horse, comfortably holding the reins. His side sheathed a short sword, and Calisto could only assume the man knew how to use it.

Beware of the wormwood and the speaker of lies.

Calisto stopped the guards and continued forward. He unfolded the blanket covering his gear and pulled his sword free. He would engage the stranger on his own and, if the man proved false, the remaining guards were to escape with the empress. Calisto had drummed this into the guards' ears before the onset of the journey. For no reason were they to come to his aid if it looked like there was trouble. Their only concern was the safety of the empress.

Calisto stopped a few meters from the stranger.

The man was slim, bordering on thin, with streaks of grey mixed with the brown of his hair. He had a pleasant and charming look on his face and would have passed for a weakling. Calisto wasn't deceived, though. He could feel the strength in the man's posture and look.

"You are here for the nail?"

"I can feel its power in that wagon, soldier. Let me pass, and I will let you leave."

"Who are you?"

"You may call me Marius."

"Deliver a message for me, scum. Tell Lucilius that I took you to hell when you meet him there."

Calisto charged at Marius and was some feet from him when Marius spoke out.

"Stop!"

Calisto pulled back on the reins of his horse, and the horse staggered to a stop. He stared in shock at Marius, for his plan had been to ride the fool down and crush him under heels. Calisto raised the sword for a killing blow.

"Stay your hand."

Calisto's swing jerked to a stop. He felt as though a force had slammed into his hand and stopped its downwards swing. Calisto strained to move his hand, and Marius smiled as he slowly got down from his horse.

"You brutes believe all matters are solved with a sword or a fist. Your life is in my hands now, foolish human. Now, take the sword to your throat and slice it slowly." Marius's words slammed into Calisto, and Calisto watched his hand holding the sword turn it around and towards his neck.

No! Calisto screamed internally. He watched Marius walk towards the wagon and the rest of the guards. His sword touched his neck, the blade cold as ice to his skin.

Beware of the wormwood and the speaker of lies.

The sword bit into his skin and a trickle of blood ran down his neck. Calisto watched helplessly as Marius reached the wagon and spoke to his guards.

Helena watched as Calisto sat rigidly on his horse and the stranger walked past him. She could sense the danger she was in and leaned out to the closest guard.

"Something is wrong. This man is a danger to us."

The guards reacted immediately and pulled out weapons from their saddles. One held a spear and rushed at the stranger.

"Stop!" It was a shout, and Helena felt the words slam into her soul. For a fraction of a second, she froze in obedience, but she shook the feeling away. She felt a pounding in her head as she broke the power of the stranger's words.

98

It must be one of the four, Helena thought as she looked at the guards in dismay.

The guard with the spear had reached the stranger. His spear tip was inches away from the heart of the stranger before the stranger spoke.

All the guards froze in place, and the stranger walked confidently through them.

"Ah, Empress Helena. I don't believe we have met. It is good to see that Myrddin isn't here with you. It seems that the gods favor me, Empress."

Helena tried to feign immobility as though she was also under the spell cast by the stranger.

"The thing with my power of persuasion, Empress, is that I know when it works. You can stop faking now and be a lady."

The stranger had walked to the wagon and leaned on it.

"Who are you?" Helena demanded.

"Ah, where are my manners! My name is Marius. At your service, your highness!" Marius gave a deep bow and smiled cunningly as he straightened himself.

There was a loud yell, and Helena heard a snapping sound. She saw the stranger stagger slightly and grimace.

"Who is this fool?" he muttered to himself. Empress Helena smiled and looked down at Marius with all the pomp her position entitled.

"My bodyguard, Calisto. I believe you two haven't met?"

Calisto yelled internally. He couldn't stop his hand from cutting into his throat. He didn't feel any pain from the nick the sword had drawn, but he knew he would still bleed out all the same.

No!

Images of his childhood flashed through his mind. The pain, loneliness, and despair of struggling to be the best. The blood and sand. He had become the champion of the arena. A man to be feared. He wasn't a lamb that could be slaughtered at a whim.

He was a lion!

Calisto roared in anger and felt the hold on his mind snap. He slumped as his will became his own again.

Never again. Never would Calisto bow in timidity and fear while evil stalked the land and reaped destruction.

Calisto felt a rage that he hadn't before. He jumped down from his horse and ran towards the wagon. Judgment was his, now.

He saw Marius standing a few feet from him with the guards surrounding him.

"You broke my hold, maggot! No one breaks my words without my permission."

Calisto stalked Marius. His rage flowed from him like a swirling mist, and Marius frowned.

"Who are you?" he asked, but Calisto remained silent. A strand of fear rose in Marius as Calisto seemed to grow before his eyes. The man remained the same, but Calisto's presence grew, and Marius shrank back in fear.

"Kill him!" he yelled at the guards as he stepped back.

Calisto saw the guards rushing towards him, but he didn't slow down. The guards seemed to be running through murky heavy water, and their movements seemed clumsy and untrained.

Calisto turned the flat of his blade and parried the spear thrust to his chest. Even though they were under the control of that snake, Marius, they were still his brothers in arms. He moved close to the guard with the spear and rendered his attack useless. Calisto struck with his blade, the flat end hitting the guard in the face.

Better to have a couple of loose teeth than an open neck.

Calisto wove through the guards.

Empress Helena watched as Calisto disarmed the guards, and in moments, they all lay groaning on the ground. She had seen Calisto fight in the arena many times and knew his prowess to be unmatched. But this looked like a different Calisto. The very air seemed to churn around him as he flowed from one guard to another.

This was grace personified.

Too soon, the fight was over, and Calisto stood over his fallen comrades. He looked around, and only then did Helena realize that Marius was gone.

The snake had escaped.

Calisto watched his guards slowly get to their feet, groaning in pain from one bruise or the other. Calisto's rage had simmered down, and he was a roaring lion that now stalked the edge of its domain. Calisto held a firm grip of his emotions and quietened his anger. The twister of lies had escaped his grasp, but Calisto hoped they would meet again.

Somehow, Merlin's words had given him the strength to break free from the hold of Marius.

Had Merlin known this would happen? Was he a seer, too?

Calisto's gaze swept the terrain looking for signs of danger. That Marius was gone wasn't a sure bet that evil wasn't lurking around the corner, waiting to bite. He turned when he heard one of the guards walk towards him.

"We are all accounted for, Captain."

Calisto nodded. It would be wise if they left the zone and made haste to their destination.

They made camp later that night in an open clearing. Calisto sat and watched as Empress Helena ate her meal. There were guards posted around the base to alert him of any danger. Empress Helena finished her meal and turned to her makeshift bed.

Calisto sighed in frustration. He had advised the empress to remain in the carriage, but she had refused. She stated that it would be safer if she sat with them. While her remarks made sense, Calisto and his guards felt uncomfortable with their empress sitting in their midst. She had asked for all their names and had praised their effort in keeping her safe.

Calisto had seen his men lift their heads higher at her words. She hadn't blamed them for falling under the spell of Marius, and for that, Calisto was grateful.

That was one reason he was happy to give his life for her. She cared for the people around her. Calisto had seen her relating with all classes of people, from the mighty to the downtrodden. Empress Helena welcomed them all with open arms. When he had tried cautioning her on the need to be circumspect, she had said it was his duty to keep her alive, but ultimately, her life was in God's hands.

Through her, Calisto had come to appreciate her God. He believed in retribution and vengeance. He was a child of war. He had accepted that years ago, but he could understand leaving his kind of life behind and following the God that preached forgiveness and love.

There was a rustling of leaves, and Calisto stretched for his sword. He saw one of his guards approach.

"How goes your watch, Titus?" The man continued towards him, and Calisto frowned. After the battle at the cavern, Calisto had agreed on coded words to identify one another. He had seen the power of the enemy and wasn't taking the safety of the empress for granted.

"Where do we rest for our weary soul?" The guard stopped a couple of feet from Calisto and looked at him. Calisto waited for an answer and got to his feet.

"Brother, I will caution you to remain still and answer the question." The remaining two guards in the camp got to their feet. Calisto quickly signaled with his fingers, and the guards moved to the empress's side.

"Who are you?" Calisto asked.

"I have a message for you, soldier," the guard spoke, but Calisto didn't recognize his voice. Swiftly, Calisto's sword was at the guard's neck.

"Go ahead and kill him. I will only find another and take over his mind." The guard chuckled and waited for Calisto's response.

Calisto looked around. Marius was nearby and had taken control of his guard. He signaled again, and one of the guards tapped Empress Helena awake.

"Speak, you deceiver of men."

"How do you come up with such terrible names? I am only here to tell you to take your sword and leave here if you value your life. The woman doesn't deserve your loyalty, soldier."

Calisto gritted his teeth in anger.

"What do you know about loyalty? All you have is lies. All you think about is falsehood. Release my brother, and maybe when I catch you, I may spare your life."

The guard chuckled again. "So savage and full of yourself because you can swing a sword. I have laid waste to men greater than you. Leave now, or I will make your life a living hell. I will destroy all that you hold dear. Everyone you love, I will either kill or make you kill them. Your friends will betray you, and you'll always wonder if it was me."

Calisto's hand blurred, and the pommel of his sword slammed into the guard's temple. The guard dropped like a sack of rice.

"I assume the guards posted to sentry duty have been compromised." Calisto walked to his empress and took a defensive position beside her.

One guard was down, which left two more guards. He didn't know the extent of Marius's power, but his words were binding. Could he control through a proxy? Calisto wasn't sure, or the conversation he had just had would have been different. He could have gone to the other guards and controlled them. The fact that he wanted Calisto to leave Empress Helena meant there was a limit to his power.

A sound from the south had Calisto spinning around. Another guard walked into the camp.

"Halt there!" Calisto commanded. The guard looked at him with a frown but stopped.

"What is wrong, Captain?"

"Where do we rest for our weary souls?" Calisto watched the guard intently.

"The Barking Inn." The guard looked confused.

Calisto relaxed. The inn was a meeting point for information sharing and rest. They were still safe.

Helena woke as the guard tapped her gently. She quickly surveyed her surroundings, trying to understand the reason for interrupting her sleep. She saw Calisto talking to a guard and then slam the pommel of his sword across the guard's head.

They were in trouble.

She couldn't see any danger, yet she trusted her bodyguard's instincts without a doubt. If Calisto felt there was trouble, then there was trouble.

Another guard came into the camp, and Calisto called out to him. The guard answered with the password and walked into the camp. The guard walked towards Calisto, and Helena saw his eyes as he passed her.

A smoky black film covered the guard's eyes. Helena realized that she could also see a thin cloud of blackness surrounding the guard.

"He is possessed," Helena shouted.

Calisto heard Empress Helena shout and reacted swiftly. He saw the guard snatch his sword and rush at him. Calisto didn't hesitate, as he had been ready for any surprise. He rushed to the guard and pushed back the guard's sword into the sheath. The guard looked at Calisto in surprise as Calisto slammed the pommel of his sword into the guard's head.

The guard had good reflexes, and the blow that would have knocked him out brushed the side of his head. But Calisto wasn't done. Still gripping the guard's hand with the sword, Calisto drove his head into the guard's face. The guard staggered and fell to his knees. A swift rap to the side of the head with his sword and the guard collapsed.

"We move now," Calisto commanded. The two guards rushed to gather the empress's bedroll, and they scrambled to get out of the clearing.

N

CHAPTER FIFTEEN

Gen opened her eyes slowly. She felt better. Her granddad sat on the chair in a pensive posture with his eyes closed. Mark sat on the floor by the door. He looked at her and smiled.

Gen returned his smile.

"How are you feeling?"

"Good. Sorry to deprive you of your bed."

"It's okay. It was a lumpy bed anyway."

Gen smiled again. She seemed to do that whenever she was in Mark's presence. She turned to her granddad.

"Is he sleeping?"

"I don't think so. Your grandfather is always aware of his surroundings."

Myrddin opened his eyes and looked at Gen. "Ready to try again?"

"I guess so, Granddad."

Myrddin nodded. "Remember, focus on the whereabouts of the other nail. Don't lose yourself to the vision."

Gen nodded again as Mark got to his feet and walked to the bed. He sat beside her. "If you feel pressured in any way, come back immediately. You can adapt in short phases."

Gen looked at Mark and then Myrddin. She felt safe and comfortable in their presence.

"Thanks, guys."

Gen turned to the nail by the other side of the bed.

She was as ready as she could ever be, and before Gen had time to second-guess herself, she grabbed the nail.

Gen was getting used to the dry air and dusty terrain. She quickly looked around her and spotted a group of people with a now-familiar figure in their midst. They seemed to be in the middle of a conversation, and Gen hurried over.

"Why do you look surprised that the fig tree has dried up?" Jesus asked his disciples.

"Have faith in God Almighty. And I can assure you that if any one of you were to say to this mountain, *be removed and cast into the sea,* and doesn't doubt it in his heart but believes that what he says with strength shall come to pass, and it shall happen for that person."

The disciples looked at Jesus in amazement. Gen stopped to study the withered fig tree as Jesus and His disciples continued their journey.

The tree looked like a dry husk about to disintegrate to dust at the slightest touch. There were no leaves on the tree or around the tree. None that Gen could see.

Gen watched Jesus and the disciples pass and wished she could follow.

She needed to focus.

She imagined reaching out with her senses to the other nail. She knew what the nail looked like, could imagine what it felt like with its rough metallic feel against her fingers.

At first, nothing happened, but Gen waited patiently.

The sensation came as a tug in her soul.

Like knowing the direction home, she could sense the other nail.

❖

Gen opened her eyes and smiled.

"I can feel it. I know where the nail is."

Mark put a hand on her shoulder gently. "Now, we make our move."

"What direction is it, Gen?" Myrddin asked.

"Give me a minute." Gen closed her eyes and focused.

She still felt the tugging sensation in her soul.

"I can feel it, but I need to locate it in our space."

"What does that even mean?"

"I can't really explain it, Mark. Just give me a sec."

Mark kept quiet and watched Gen as she concentrated.

A smile crept across her lips a while later, and she opened her eyes.

"Got it! It's here in Saskatoon. By a playground…no, maybe a park or something."

Gen looked at Myrddin and Mark and shrugged her shoulders.

"I could take you…"

"No way."

"Out of the question," Mark and Myrddin both interrupted Gen.

Mark brought out his phone.

"A playground or park, right? How far do you think it is? Can you even do that?"

"The impression I got wasn't too far."

"Okay, we have three playgrounds slash parks close to us." Mark showed Gen a picture of a playground, and she shook her head after a glance. Mark flipped to another image, and her eyes lit up.

"That's it! The other nail is in that vicinity."

"Good." Myrddin stood up.

"I still think Mark should follow you, Granddad."

"I can handle myself."

"Just be careful."

Myrddin smiled at Gen and Mark and headed for the door.

"You're not going to…you know." Mark waved his hand in a circular motion.

"What do you take me for?" Myrddin asked with a twinkle in his eyes. "Haven't you heard of Uber?"

Gen hugged her granddad and watched as he left the motel room.

"He'll be okay, Gen. He's the Merlin."

"He's still my granddad."

Mark acknowledged that fact in silence and watched as Gen paced the room.

"The pacing part normally comes some hours after sitting down and worrying, you know."

Gen looked up to see Mark smiling softly.

"These guys have been around for ages."

"So has your granddad. And if the legend is true, he's no pushover. He'll be all right, Gen."

Gen nodded.

He had to be all right.

Mr. Isherwood drove the pickup van slowly into 'Triple 7' ranch.

There was the sound of crunching gravel as the van glided to a stop, breaking the silence. Mrs. Isherwood opened her eyes when she felt the van coast to a halt. The beam from the headlights pierced the darkness of the night as she looked at the house and noticed the sheriff's van parked in front of it.

"Is that Liam?" Mr. Isherwood squinted while adjusting his glasses.

"No, dear, that's Theo. And is our front door open?"

Mrs. Isherwood stared at the gaping hole where the door should be. They watched as Theo walked towards them.

"Mr. Isherwood. Mrs. Isherwood," Theo greeted.

Mrs. Isherwood frowned at Theo's formal tone.

"What's going on, Theo?"

"Have you heard from Genesis, ma'am?"

"Genesis? What's happening, Theo?"

"We need to know if you've been in contact with your daughter, ma'am."

"Eh…we …we were with her this morning. Had breakfast. What's wrong with my daughter, Theo?"

Theo stopped by their van and put a hand on the hood of the driver's side.

"So, you haven't heard from her since this morning?"

"Is she in some kind of trouble, young man?" Mr. Isherwood demanded.

"I'm not at liberty to say, sir. Should you come into contact with her, kindly inform the sheriff's office."

Mr. and Mrs. Isherwood stared as Theo headed back to his car and drove off. Their gaze turned to the gaping hole in front of their house. They wondered what could have caused that.

The park was more of an open field with clusters of shrubs and small trees. There was a seesaw in a clearing and a swing for the kids.

Myrddin walked into the park and sensed the presence of the nail.

"You're not making this tough, Atticus," Myrddin spoke out.

Atticus stepped out from behind a tree and walked towards Myrddin.

"We sensed your feeble attempt at scrying, charlatan, and decided to welcome you."

"That wasn't me, but that is neither here nor there."

Atticus frowned.

"So, this is a trap? Doesn't look like much. Knowing the coward that you are, you didn't come alone, did you?" Atticus hissed in anger, and Myrddin smiled.

"I had walked upon this earth before you were even thought of being—"

"Here we go again, Atticus. I must say, you think too highly of yourself. I sense two of you here. Please come out. Let's get this over with."

There was a rustling from Myrddin's left, and a man in his mid-thirties stepped out. He was slim, almost bordering on lanky with a goatee and a smile.

"Ah, Remus. It has been a while. You carry a different face but still smell the same. That, you cannot hide."

"Myrddin." Remus tipped his head in greeting.

"Still as cocky and arrogant as ever. That has been your greatest flaw."

"I see it as being as truthful as ever, Remus."

"You are strong, Myrddin, I grant you that, but you cannot defeat both of us."

Myrddin saw a young couple come out of the bushes some meters from them. They paused when they realized they weren't alone but ran off when Myrddin allowed an arc of static energy to become visible around his right hand.

"I am only here for the nail, Atticus. It has long been in your possession. I think it's time it was returned."

"Oh, Myrddin, Myrddin. We didn't only set this trap for you. By now, Lucilius will have found the nail. All three will soon be in our possession, as they should be. It seems a certain young deputy blames the keeper for recent incidents. We know where the girl is, Myrddin."

Atticus gestured his hand in a quick intricate pattern, and Myrddin felt a thrum of power.

"Really, Atticus? A containment spell?"

A containment spell effectively enclosed an area from outside influence. The flip side to the spell was that it also caged the people inside from leaving unless the user released the magic.

Myrddin felt the power of the containment spell, but he could easily break it.

As Myrddin thought through his situation, Remus revealed a bow in his hand with an arrow nocked. Remus aimed and released, the arrow flying rapidly towards Myrddin.

Myrddin grimaced in annoyance.

He had two choices. He could fight Atticus and Remus and take the nail from them, or he could break the spell and head back to Gen and Mark.

Gen and Mark needed his help.

Myrddin created a field to stop the arrow's flight and was surprised as the arrow broke through. Myrddin shifted to the side, the arrow missing his heart by a narrow margin.

That shouldn't be able to happen, Myrddin thought as the arrow grazed his ribs, tearing through cloth with ease.

"Surprised, Myrddin?" Atticus gloated as Remus nocked another arrow.

"You see, over the years, we've had the time to experiment with the nail. While the nail can kill us, we need to have the three in our possession.

It seems since we were cursed to roam this earth together, we can only leave together."

"What we found, though, was that the nail could cause incredible pain. It can dismember and cut off our limbs. We couldn't remold the nail as we needed it, but even little scraps of fillings from it can still be very potent. No magic can withstand it."

Myrddin recognized the smell emanating from the arrow in Remus's hands. He had thought it was from the nail, and while he had been correct, he had been deflected by that fact.

Remus released another arrow at Myrddin and swiftly nocked another, while Atticus sent a lightning bolt at Myrddin.

Myrddin felt the arrow coming and created a blade of compressed air.

Magic was a thing of the mind. Over the years, Myrddin had come to realize that for practical magic, he needed a focus.

For him, one verse from scripture enabled his mind to become razor-sharp.

No weapon formed or fashioned against me shall prosper.

Myrddin moved, almost in a blur. His blade sliced cleanly through the shaft of the arrow, and he flicked his left hand, deflecting Atticus's lightning attack towards Remus.

Remus dodged the lightning bolt and released another arrow at Myrddin. Myrddin shot a gust of wind at Remus and shifted his aim at the last minute, making the arrow fly above his head.

Myrddin clapped his hand, and a sonic boom radiated. The next arrow shattered before leaving Remus's bow. Atticus grunted and staggered back as the sonic boom hit him. He prepared another lightning bolt, but Myrddin disappeared.

"He can't leave this containment without revealing himself," Atticus shouted.

Atticus and Remus felt the leaves and shrubs flutter as a breeze blew them away.

They looked up to see Myrddin descending from above, a tornado gathering around him.

Gen looked out of the motel bedroom window. She frowned as she saw flashes of lightning light up the sky in the distance.

Was her granddad all right?

She knew she shouldn't be worried, but she couldn't help herself.

109

Another bolt of lightning lit the night sky, and Gen gasped in alarm as the lightning revealed the silhouette of a man standing in the motel parking lot.

There was something about the man that Gen didn't like. He seemed to suck the shadows around him into himself.

"Mark?"

Mark rushed to the window and looked out.

"What is it?"

Gen looked again, but the parking lot was empty.

"I thought...must be my mind."

"What did you see, Gen?"

Mark turned Gen to face him. Gen frowned as she recalled the man she had seen.

"For a minute, I thought I saw someone standing in the parking lot."

"What did he look like?"

Gen looked at Mark and was glad that he was taking her seriously. It could have been her imagination.

"Maybe it was my imagination."

"Maybe, maybe not."

"I saw a shadow standing there for a moment. The man just looked... wrong, I guess."

"That's good enough for me. Let's get out of here."

Mark headed to the door when the lights flickered.

He picked up the M4 from the table and aimed at the door. He took a deep breath and focused, his finger brushing the trigger, waiting.

The door burst open, and Mark pulled the trigger, a burst of bullets spraying the doorway.

Mark watched in amazement as a stranger rushed into the room.

He was in his mid-forties with a scar over one of his eyes. The stranger held a sword and did the impossible — he sliced the bullet aiming for his heart as he dodged and weaved around the doorway.

From the information Myrddin had given him, Mark knew the stranger could only be Lucilius, which meant that Gen was in danger. He advanced towards the stranger.

Mark aimed again and shot at Lucilius, who used his blade's flat side to deflect the bullet away. Lucilius entered his guard, but Mark remained focused and undeterred.

This was a fight he knew.

Mark saw the blade of Lucilius's sword sweep for his throat, and he ducked under the swing, his hands tucking in to pull his M4 closer to his chest.

Most people thought getting close to a person holding a rifle rendered the rifle user useless.

Most people thought wrong.

Mark shot from his hips as he aimed his tilted gun at Lucilius's head. Mark was fast, making decisions out of training honed from years of combat.

Lucilius was faster, though.

Lucilius moved his head a fraction, and the bullet whisked away. He struck at Mark's heart with the tip of the blade, and Mark blocked with the barrel of his gun.

Gen watched the fight. She was scared to move for fear of breaking Mark's concentration. Mark and Lucilius seemed to be dancing partners, each entering the other's guard and striking.

It was as amazing as it was deadly. One mistake would spell the end for the other.

The sword whisked over Mark's head. He saw Lucilius kick at him, and he had no choice but to take it. Moving away would bring him into Lucilius's killing zone. Mark bent and took the kick with his shoulder, absorbing the impact. He had a couple of bullets left, so he needed to make them count.

Mark had leaned a little forward into the kick, so Lucilius was unbalanced, and Mark moved in. He rose from his bent position and shoved Lucilius back, aiming his carbine at Lucilius's head.

Lucilius fell back and, in one clean motion, cut off the nozzle of Mark's M4. Mark stared at his cut gun in surprise.

What the...

He hesitated a second too long, and Lucilius moved in for the kill.

He stabbed at Mark's heart.

Mark heard Gen scream in fear as Lucilius's sword pierced his Kevlar. Mark dropped his M4 and gripped the blade of the sword with his gloved hand.

For a moment, the sword stuck as he held it firm, and he looked into Lucilius's eye. Mark saw a flicker of surprise pass over Lucilius's face.

Mark quickly pulled his Glock from his hip holster and shot Lucilius in the heart. The motion was fluid and smooth, a decision made from reflex and deadly instinct. Mark pulled the trigger repeatedly until the gun clicked empty.

Lucilius staggered and hit the bedroom wall with a thud. He slumped to the floor and lay still.

"Is he dead?" Gen whispered.

She couldn't believe her eyes. For a moment, she thought Lucilius had stabbed Mark. She had never seen anything like what she'd just witnessed. Gen had suspected Mark was highly trained from the way he carried himself. He seemed to prowl and had an intimidating air, but this? *This* was exceptional.

Mark ejected the empty clip and searched in his pocket for another.

"From what Myrddin said, I don't think we can really..."

Lucilius took a deep breath and opened his eye. Gen screamed again as Lucilius leaped to his feet and grabbed Mark by the throat.

"I will enjoy ripping your head from your miserable body," Lucilius bellowed.

Mark didn't struggle with Lucilius as he felt the grip on his throat tighten. He knew he probably had a couple of seconds before Lucilius snapped his neck like a twig.

Mark made those seconds count. He inserted a fresh magazine into his Glock and shoved it under Lucilius's chin.

"Let's see you grow a new brain, cyclops."

Mark pulled the trigger.

He knew Lucilius would be hard to kill but recovering from having your brains scattered would surely hurt like hell.

Lucilius moved in a blur. He squeezed the nozzle of the Glock and crushed it, blocking the chamber. The gun exploded.

Mark saw the Glock 45's nozzle crumble under Lucilius's grip and shielded his face from the explosion as Lucilius dropped him to avoid being hurt by the pieces of metal flying about.

The gun exploded, sending fragments and particles scattering across the room. Mark fell and rolled backward, creating distance between him and Lucilius. His throat hurt, and he found it difficult to breathe. He sprang to his feet and felt Lucilius barrel into him. Mark fell on the bed and felt a sharp pain in his right side.

Mark groaned in agony as he looked at Lucilius standing above him. Lucilius held the pommel of his sword, and Mark traced it to see the other end sticking in his own body.

Mark turned to Gen, who stood frozen in disbelief.

"Run," Mark whispered.

Gen looked at the door, but Lucilius shook his finger at her.

"Not this time, keeper. This dance is over. Now, hand me the nail."

Gen stared into Lucilius's cold eye. Death stared back at her.

Gen shook her head weakly. She wasn't going to hand the nail to this monster.

❖

Myrddin landed with a boom, creating a crater around him. Atticus and Remus were blasted away by the power Myrddin emitted. Remus slammed against a tree and slumped to the ground.

Atticus weathered the storm, grunting in pain as air shredded his clothes and grated his skin.

Myrddin gathered more power and released it. The containment field around the area shattered into a thousand pieces. He thrummed with energy as he looked at Atticus and the fallen Remus.

"Hope we don't meet again, Atticus. I assure you that I won't be so gentle."

Atticus let go of his held breath as Myrddin vanished again.

CHAPTER SIXTEEN

Gen watched as Lucilius walked calmly towards her. She had backed up against the wall and had nowhere to go. She heard Mark groan in pain as he struggled vainly to pull out the sword pinning him to the bed.

"This looks very familiar, keeper. It seems that dying is all that your protectors do." He smiled grimly and extended his hand.

"Hand it over, or I will extract it from your corpse. I will not ask again."

Gen shook her head again. Her heart beat so rapidly, she was surprised she hadn't passed out yet.

"You will never have it."

If she was going to die, she might as well spit in the face of evil. For the man standing before her was pure malice.

The darkness swirled around him as he stopped a few inches from Gen. A darkness so dark it sucked the light from the bedroom.

From the corner of her eye, she saw Mark dig into his pocket for a weapon in a frantic bid to help her, and she almost broke down in tears.

He was dying because of her.

Suddenly, the bulbs flickered again and blew up, sending shimmering sparks around the room. The showers looked like golden snowflakes, and Gen covered her eyes with the back of her palm to avoid any sparks getting in her eyes.

Myrddin appeared out of nowhere. He blazed so much power that though Gen shut her eyes, they still hurt from the afterburn of his image.

Lucilius screamed in pain from the light emitting from Myrddin. He grabbed Gen and spun her around, using her as a shield against Myrddin's brightness.

Lucilius held Gen in a tight grip, one of his hands around her throat.

"Release her, and maybe you walk out of here on your feet," Myrddin's voice boomed. He didn't shout, but his voice rippled across the room and slammed into Lucilius.

The air in the room warped from the power rippling out of Myrddin.

Gen felt Lucilius's fear as he faced the might of the greatest enchanter ever to live.

Gen glanced at Mark and saw that he wasn't moving.

Hold on. Please don't die.

"Save him grand…" She was interrupted by the appearance of Atticus. He materialized beside her and Lucilius. He stared in concentration as he tried to hold on to the power enabling him to teleport.

Lucilius grabbed Gen and moved to Atticus. He touched his shoulder, and they winked out of existence.

❖

Myrddin looked at Mark lying on the bed. He could feel Mark's life slowly bleeding away. He walked up to him, and Mark opened his eyes. Myrddin saw the effort it took him to remain conscious.

"You need to go after them. You need to get Gen back," Mark groaned. He wouldn't last long before he faded away, his spirit rising to the clouds to await judgment.

Not yet, soldier.

Myrddin stood with one leg on the bed and grasped the sword. Mark moaned, too weak to shout.

"This is going to hurt, but I need to take it out."

Mark nodded slowly. Myrddin yanked the sword out, and Mark moaned in agony. The bed was soaked with his blood as Myrddin leaned forward and rested his hand on Mark's torso. Myrddin concentrated, and power flowed through him into the wound.

Supernatural healing wasn't his strong point, but he had enough to bring Mark back from the brink of death.

Mark gasped and slowly sat upright. The room spun around him as he tried to reorientate his mind to the moment. He was spent, barely conscious, but Mark summoned the energy to remain sitting. He peered through the tear the sword had made through his clothes to look at the wound. Myrddin had somehow accelerated the healing process, and Mark could see the result. The injury wasn't completely healed, but Mark could move. That was enough for him.

"Do you know where they are?" he asked, his voice raspy and weak.

Myrddin grunted in reply and sat down. He felt utterly exhausted. He had expended more spiritual energy than he had in centuries.

Power had its cost, and for him, it was his life essence. He felt a little lightheaded, but he knew the feeling would pass with rest and a good meal — something they couldn't afford right now.

"They are heading towards Dundurn."

"Then that's where we go. I'm sure Lucilius will be greatly surprised when they realize they don't have what they want," Mark grunted as he bent down and retrieved an object from under the bed.

Myrddin sat up and smiled.

"You have been a busy young man."

Mark dropped the handkerchief on the bed and unfolded it. They stared at the third nail.

"It was Gen's idea. She figured they wouldn't notice if the nail was on her or somewhere close by. It was supposed to be for insurance."

"This is good, Mark. It will buy us some time, so I can find them."

Mark looked at Myrddin. "I'm coming."

"You are hurt," Myrddin said.

"You are spent," Mark countered.

Myrddin raised an eyebrow, and Mark shrugged.

"I see things, little details that help me survive in my line of work."

Myrddin nodded.

"You know if you join me, there is the possibility that you'll re-encounter Lucilius."

"I'm aware of that."

"Do you know why he likes swords?"

"He enjoys sticking people with them?" Mark joked. His side still hurt, though it was now a muted pain.

"Lucilius believes in the challenge, the hunt for mastery, and to be the best. For him, a sword is personal. It shows his skill as an individual."

"He has me at a disadvantage there. I saw him cut through bullets. Was that magic?"

"Experience. And having an enchanted sword." Myrddin picked up Lucilius's sword and balanced it in his hands.

"Atticus cast a spell for durability, anti-wear, and a sharp edge. I've done the same to some objects over the years."

"Wait, are we talking about—"

"I can show you someone to help bridge the gap between you two," Myrddin interrupted. They didn't have the time to be sidetracked by his earlier escapes in life.

"A swordmaster? We don't have that kind of time. We need to get to Gen quickly."

"I thought you liked being prepared."

"And there is a time for haste. This is such a time."

Myrddin smiled.

"I assure you that knowledge is your greatest weapon. Understanding of a thing our one desire."

Mark frowned at Myrddin. It was apparent that he spoke about a totally different matter, but Mark couldn't place it.

Why should understanding be our one desire?

He watched warily as Myrddin walked to him and placed his hands on both sides of his head, just above his ears.

"See! I grant unto you wisdom and understanding."

Mark felt his mind explode. Kaleidoscopic images rushed through his mind, and it took him a while to sort through them or understand them.

He saw a young boy walk into the middle of a crowd.

The air was dry, and he could feel the sand underneath the boy's feet. The place looked like a training ground with wooden half-figures erected at a corner.

There were other boys his age, while some were older. The boy was naked except for the loin cloth around his groin. Someone handed the boy a wooden sword, and the boy balanced the sword in his hand.

Another boy walked into the circle, also holding a wooden sword, and they squared off.

They hacked and slashed at each other without finesse or style, both grunting and struggling with fatigue. The wooden sword felt like lead in the child's hands, but the boy held on to it for dear life.

The clacking sound filled the arena, and the two boys separated. With a yell, the boy charged the other and swung repeatedly. He put all his strength into the swing. The boy eventually hit his opponent on the side of the head with the wooden sword and his opponent fell to the floor.

Another boy rushed in and swung a wooden sword at the boy. The boy barely moved his head out of the way. The boy looked at his next opponent in exhaustion. He could barely move his hands, and he had to move back to avoid the swing of the wooden sword from the second boy. His opponent grinned as he saw the state the boy was in.

The boy stood and watched as the bigger boy rushed into his guard, swinging wildly. He sacrificed a blow to his shoulder and blinked as tears stung his eyes. Summoning his remaining strength, the boy jabbed straight with his sword and hit the other boy in the center of his head. The second boy fell like a log.

The boy heard footsteps rushing towards him but couldn't respond. He felt the air displace as a wooden sword aimed for his head. The last thing he heard before he passed out from the blow was the other children chanting his name.

The images fast-forwarded, and Mark saw the boy had become a teenager now. The boy had grown into a tall, lean young man with muscles that were firm and rippled as he held his wooden sword.

The teenager was in the same training ground in a circle, but he faced three opponents. Two held similar wooden swords, while the third had a wooden shield and a sword.

The three opponents came at the teenager at once, trying to surround him and beat him down.

The teenager moved with a grace that surprised Mark. He stepped aside as a wooden sword slashed for his head. The teenager spun and stuck at the man with the wooden shield, the teenager's sword extended out in a straight aim. The impact drove the man with the wooden shield backward, and the teenager moved at the opponent to his right.

The teenager's moves were fluid and precise, devoid of excess swings and motions.

He lashed out and struck one of his opponents in the chest. The man groaned in pain and dropped to the sand. In the same motion, the teenager ducked as the third man swung his sword at his neck.

The teenager moved swiftly into the man's space and jabbed him under the armpit of the hand holding the wooden sword. The last man standing rushed at the teenager with his shield. The teenager dived to the side and rolled, coming up smoothly, and swiped his sword at the opponent's exposed back. The strike's force drove his opponent to the ground, and when the man looked up, the teenager's sword was at the man's neck.

The fight was over.

The teenager turned as the crowd around him yelled his name.

"Calisto! Calisto! Calisto!"

Images flashed through Mark's mind in an instant. Sword forms and style as Calisto trained over the years.

The images settled again, and Mark saw Myrddin bent over a dying Calisto. Calisto clutched a mortal wound in his stomach as Myrddin leaned down and whispered in his ear.

"Have no fear, warrior, for your empress shall always have a protector. You will live and have a son. You shall call him Mart-kos, for he shall be a warrior and protector."

Myrddin placed his hand on Calisto's wound, and Calisto gasped as he felt power flow through him.

❖

Mark gasped as Myrddin removed his hands from his head. He steadied his breathing and tried to make sense of the images he had seen.

Had that been his ancestor? Myrddin had said that his lineage had always protected the keeper of the nails.

Mark saw an object sail towards him, and he reached out instinctively. He caught the sword by the pommel and swung it in a full circle, the swishing sound a comfort to his soul.

"I take it you met your ancestor."

Mark nodded, engrossed in his new talent.

The sword felt right in his hand. Not a dagger, but not wholly a broad blade, either.

A perfect balance.

"I think it's time to get our keeper back," Mark said and looked at Myrddin.

Myrddin smiled.

❖

Gen sat in the back of the black SUV, sandwiched between Atticus and Lucilius. Gen hadn't seen the young man before driving the car, but she knew he was one of the four.

They all exuded the same darkness.

She felt smothered by it.

Atticus's spell hadn't precisely been a teleporting spell but more like a cloaking one. They had still been in the room but hidden from every sight, including Myrddin.

Atticus and Lucilius had quickly rushed from the motel room, probably sensing that her granddad would have seen through their little masquerade.

An SUV van had been waiting by the roadside, and they had huddled inside, dragging Gen with them.

Gen prayed that Mark was all right. She had been thankful when she had seen her granddad. Knowing who he was now, she was confident that he would be able to do something to stop Mark from dying.

Having lived all these centuries, he must have picked up a spell or two.

"Where is the nail, keeper? What have you done? I cannot sense its proximity." Lucilius glared at Gen.

Atticus frowned and searched Gen.

"It's not on her."

"I know. Where is it?"

"Where you will never get your hands on it," Gen taunted.

Atticus closed his eyes and muttered beneath his breath. He opened them some seconds later.

"It's still at the last location. She must have dropped it somehow."

"Then Myrddin has it," Lucilius stated.

Gen watched Lucilius and Atticus exchange a glance, and Atticus nodded.

"To the ranch, Remus. We have a deal to trade."

Gen was worried, but she wasn't scared of the people inside the van.

They were evil, and that was plain to see, but she knew they lusted after the foot nail, and as long as it wasn't with her, she was safe.

At least she hoped she was safe.

She watched as they drove into the town of Dundurn. Her town. It was still the early morning hours, and the city was peaceful as the residents slept, unaware of the evil that had come into their midst.

They turned into 'Triple 7' ranch, and Gen's heart lurched in her chest as she saw her parents' truck.

The black SUV parked, and Atticus dragged Gen out.

She saw her mum run out of the house and head towards them.

"Mum, get back."

Her mum stopped a few feet from the group and looked at Gen.

"Who are these men, honey?"

"Please, Mum, you need to get back into the house."

Her father came out of the house, and to Gen's surprise, he held a rifle.

"Are you okay, Genesis?"

Gen stared with her mouth open at her dad. Gone was the dorky look. He still had on his glasses, but there was nothing weak about him.

"Lower your weapon, Isherwood. You wouldn't want anything to happen to the keeper now, would you?" Lucilius threatened.

"I know what you are, spawn of hell. Let my daughter go before you feel buckshot in your face," Gen's dad demanded.

"If you know what I am, then you know that your puny weapon will only be a distraction. We are not here for you." Lucilius released his hold on Gen's arm, and she rushed into her mother's arms.

"Are you okay, honey?" her mum asked.

Gen nodded and watched her dad, who still had the gun pointed at Lucilius's head.

"Myrddin will be here soon," Atticus said

"Then we'd better have the appropriate welcome ready for him." Lucilius looked at Gen's father. "There is a limit to my patience, and I won't repeat myself."

"Dad, put the gun down. It will only irritate them."

Gen's dad reluctantly lowered his gun and watched as the men walked his daughter into the house.

CHAPTER SEVENTEEN

Mark walked down the road with Myrddin by his side.

They had driven their rented car into town but had decided to park the car some distance away from the ranch. Mark had thought of various scenarios and plans but decided to go with the straightforward approach.

When in doubt, walk through the front door. Or, in this case, the front gate.

Mark and Myrddin had agreed that Lucilius and his colleagues knew that they were coming. They also decided that some type of trap would be laid, so they decided to pay them back in their own coin.

Mark was under a guise. An invisible spell that caused him to move about unseen. Myrddin wasn't sure if Atticus would sense him, but Mark felt the element of surprise would still be on their side.

Myrddin held Lucilius's sword wrapped in a torn bedsheet, the part they could tear that wasn't soaked with blood. His blood. His wound throbbed at his side, reminding him of his brush with death.

Myrddin had said that the invisible spell could only work on him and that the sword was anathema to his magic.

They reached the 'Triple 7' ranch and walked in. Mark noted the black SUV, the trademark of Lucilius and his goons. He also saw Gen's parents' truck, and he frowned.

He hoped they weren't around.

Myrddin stood close to the road and looked around.

"Atticus has erected another containment spell. That's good."

"How is that? And what is a containment spell?"

"We can handle our business without fear of the residents being aware. It contains sound and living things that enter the field." Mark digested the information in silence. He looked around the ranch but couldn't see anything out of the ordinary.

That didn't mean they weren't waiting for them, though.

"So, what do you sense?" He knew Myrddin wasn't just standing by the road for the fun of it. "Is Gen here?"

"She is," Myrddin confirmed. "But so are her parents. That is unexpected."

Mark grunted. They would have to adjust their plan, but he wasn't worried. He always entered an operation with an open mind. Plan but always be flexible and compensate for the unexpected. Mark fleetingly wondered what his drill sergeant would make of this.

"What of Lucilius?"

"He is here," Myrddin said. "And so are the others. They also brought reinforcements."

"How many?"

"Enough to be a distraction. We have guards in the barn and behind the house. Hoping to box us in."

"So, what's the play?"

"There's a sniper in the barn with two other guards. Lucilius is in the house with the others and four guards at the back."

"Okay, stall them. I'll make a sweep through the barn and the back of the house."

Mark didn't have any guns on him, but he was confident he could handle the guards.

He jogged to the barn as Myrddin walked to the house.

He noticed the barn door was ajar and slowly crept in. The barn was in darkness, but Mark caught the muffled sound of someone breathing by his left.

One guard.

He looked around. To make the trap effective, there should be another guard right about—

Mark spotted the second guard on his right, hidden amongst Myrddin's work tools. Mark walked deeper into the barn. He needed to find the sniper.

If he could take out the sniper quietly, he would be armed.

Mark saw a ladder leaning against the loft of the barn. A perfect place to see the main house from the opened window.

Mark crept slowly, balancing himself on the soles of his feet. He climbed the ladder and winced as it creaked from his weight. He could feel eyes turned in his direction, but Mark was confident that he remained invisible.

Myrddin's spells wouldn't be weak or easily detected, at least not by these individuals. Mark waited a couple of seconds and continued climbing. He reached the loft and froze.

Mark stared into the extended barrel of a gun.

The sniper with a Barrett M82 rifle swept the loft slowly, looking for an intruder.

Mark remained still. He knew the sniper couldn't see him, but Myrddin hadn't mentioned anything about Mark being silent as well.

Satisfied that there was no imminent threat, the sniper turned back to his position and looked through his telescope. Mark crept forward. He wished he had his switchblade with him.

He had to take out the sniper without any noise.

Mark was a few feet from the sniper when the man sensed his presence.

The sniper moved for his side holster when Mark jumped him. Mark gripped the hand going for the side gun with his left hand and jabbed the back of the sniper's neck with his other hand. Mark struck a pressure point adjacent to the sniper's Adam's apple, and the sniper jerked and crumbled to the ground.

Mark pulled a semi-automatic pistol with a suppressor from the side holster. He climbed back down and advanced on the guards by the door. They must have heard the scuffle, for they waved their guns as they swept the area around the ladder. The guards stayed beside each other, offering protection for one another.

It looked almost too easy, as Mark had the advantage of invisibility. He slammed the butt of the pistol into the neck of the first guard and gripped the hand of the second guard as the first slumped unconscious. The second guard tried to press the trigger, but Mark jabbed his gun at the man's throat. The man dropped his weapon, clutching at his throat. Mark hit the man on the side of the head and watched him slump to the ground.

Myrddin walked into the house and went to the living room. He immediately saw Gen tied to a chair with her parents beside her.

Sitting across from them were Lucilius, Atticus, and Remus. They seemed relaxed and smug.

Lucilius had another sword in his lap while Remus played with a golden coin.

"Good, I don't have to spend the night hunting you down," Myrddin said and turned to Gen's parents.

"Sorry about this mess, Martha. Pete, how're you holding up?"

"Been better, sir," Mr. Isherwood said.

"I take it these pricks are here for the nail, Myrddin?" Martha asked. She glared at the men across the room in distaste, and Myrddin smiled.

Gen had inherited her spirit from her mother, and Myrddin knew if looks could kill, Lucilius and the others would be long dead.

Myrddin saw the look of confusion on Gen's face and gave a slight shrug. "It's been the way of things, Gen."

Gen looked at her parents. "You know of the nails?"

"Our family has been its protectors for generations, honey. Of course we know."

That explained a lot. She now understood her parents' lack of concern or sorrow at her granddad's fake death, the glances she had seen between them but couldn't understand, and their initial reluctance to have her go to university.

"I believe you have the nail with you, Myrddin," Lucilius said.

"It's close by. I believe we are here to negotiate. Why don't we start by releasing Gen's parents? Holding them doesn't gain you much."

"On the contrary, Myrddin, her parents are a good bargaining chip to ensure the bearer's cooperation. And yours. Now hand over the nail before we begin to dismember the mother before her daughter."

"I have a better option, Lucilius. Let everybody go, and I won't make it my lifelong ambition to hunt each of you down like the dogs you are."

"Bray as much as you like, Myrddin. We have the upper hand here," Atticus gloated.

"There are three of us and one of you. I believe you desire the girl and her parents unharmed. We can give you that, but we want the nail."

Myrddin saw Gen shake her head.

"They mustn't get it, Granddad. You know how critical the nail is."

But you are even more important, Myrddin thought to himself.

He sensed Mark coming and smiled. Maybe the odds were tilting to his favor after all.

"We are at an impasse, Lucilius. You have what I need, and I have what you need. You need the nail. You don't need the girl or her parents, so let them go."

"This blather is getting tiresome," Atticus said and got to his feet. His hands twisted in an arcane spell, and he shot bolts of lightning at Gen's parents.

Mark watched as the last guard slumped to the ground, lifeless.

He had taken out the two remaining guards in the barn and had snuck to the back of the house. The four guards had been taken by surprise when Mark descended on them. Their laxity and casual stand sparked some irritation in him, and he made them suffer for it.

The invisibility spell that Myrddin had woven on him allowed anything under his clothes to remain hidden. Still, the moment he brought out the pistol he had taken from the sniper, the guards were startled to see a gun floating in midair.

Mark moved through the guards with an ease that surprised him.

He jabbed his knuckles at the throat of one guard, who staggered back, choking and trying to force air into his bruised throat. Mark slapped the butt of the gun into the face of the closest guard and bent down low. He swept the next guard off his feet, and while that guard tumbled to the ground, Mark slammed the bottom of his palm into the nose of the last guard.

The guard's nose broke, and the force of the blow slammed into his head, rendering him unconscious immediately. Mark barely broke a sweat as he saw four guards sprawled around him.

He had changed.

The knowledge lodged in his head had changed him. He was better. Able to adapt quickly to unforeseen situations. He wasn't physically stronger, but he felt more assertive in his mind. That knowledge seemed to affect the way his body responded in a fight.

Mark picked up another pistol and shoved it into his pants, the cold metal tight against his back. He moved to the back door and opened it, slowly creeping into the house. He could hear voices coming from the living room and headed that way.

N

CHAPTER EIGHTEEN

Gen screamed.

The lightning bolt arced out of Atticus's hand and raced towards her parents. Her mother's eyes opened wide as she saw the instrument of her death lash at her.

Her father didn't have time to be surprised as the lightning bolt struck and hit—

Nothing.

Or rather, something. The air around Gen's parents flashed silvery blue as the lightning bolts hit a force field around them.

Myrddin wasted no time and released a blast of wind at Atticus and the others.

Atticus's shield flared a reddish-brown as the furniture around the three of them was blown away.

"Now that we've shown our intent, can we renegotiate?" Myrddin said.

Atticus, Lucilius, and Remus were on their feet as every piece of furniture in their part of the living room gathered into a heap behind them.

"How long can you keep it up, Myrddin? I can keep attacking them all day. Hand over the nail."

Myrddin smiled, and Atticus frowned.

"About that. I did say the nail was nearby. I just never said that it was on me."

A gun appeared in midair and shot at the three of them. Atticus raised a shield around them but wasn't quick enough as Remus grunted and staggered back in pain as a bullet pierced his chest.

Lucilius swung his sword and dodged a bullet aimed at his head. Myrddin used the distraction to rush to Gen and her parents. "Outside immediately."

The remaining bullets hit Atticus's shield.

Martha nodded and dragged her husband quickly towards the door. Atticus had seen Gen's parents escaping and sent another bolt of lightning at them. A silver tray flew in the air and intercepted the bolt, sending it spiraling to the ceiling.

The gun in the air barked again, and Atticus slapped the bullet aside in irritation.

Someone was disguised.

Atticus quickly chanted and shouted. "Reveal!"

His spell washed over the whole room, and Mark's invisibility spell was broken.

Mark flung the tray at Atticus as he saw that he was no longer hidden from their sight. He watched from the corner of his eye as Myrddin untied Gen. Her parents had almost reached the door when Lucilius rushed at them.

Mark moved to intercept. He saw an object sail in the air and snatched Lucilius's former sword from the air. Lucilius stopped a few feet away from Mark and looked at the sword in his hand.

"I believe that belongs to me," he said as his gaze fell on the sword.

"You know what they say about finders being keepers and all that. I applaud your taste in swords, by the way."

Lucilius tilted his head as he observed Mark.

"You should be dead."

"I know, but these past few days have been strange. You should be dead, too."

"I am immortal. I cannot be dead. And I can see that you're not fully healed from our last encounter. How do you expect to win?"

"I've been thinking about that. You may be immortal, but you can be hurt. You bleed. My plan is quite simple. Cut you into a thousand pieces and scatter you to the four winds. Let's see how you come back from that."

"A very ambitious plan." Lucilius seemed to be amused. "But tell me, how do you expect to cut me?"

"With this sword, dear Lucilius, with this sword."

Mark moved in swiftly, and their swords clashed.

Myrddin created a thin blade of wind and sliced the ropes binding Gen. He watched from the corner of his eye as Remus got to his feet, completely healed from the gunshot wound. Atticus released another bolt of lightning, and Myrddin slapped it away.

Gen's parents had made it out of the living room, and Myrddin could sense them outside the house.

Mark's arrival had been impeccable.

128

He had sensed the moment of surprise on Lucilius and Atticus's faces. The odds were about even now.

"Go to your parents, Gen."

"I can help."

"Not here and not now. Don't worry about Mark. He can handle himself." Myrddin knew Lucilius was a formidable foe, but his desire for single combat meant he didn't have to worry about him interfering. Whatever happened, Myrddin had to make sure none of them escaped the house. This was the first time in eons that the possibility of hurting or even killing the accursed had presented itself. He couldn't afford to waste the opportunity.

"Gen, you need to go."

Gen reluctantly agreed and made for the door.

Gen made for the door but couldn't help stopping to watch Mark and Lucilius fight. She was scared for Mark as she remembered the ease with which Lucilius had seriously wounded him the last time. As she watched, she noticed that there was something different about Mark.

He had changed, and Gen frowned.

She could also see a glow around him. Faint and hardly visible but present all the same. As Lucilius was enshrouded in darkness, Mark seemed to pulse with light.

What had happened to him?

Mark moved like the wind. He darted in and out, measuring, gauging Lucilius's responses. Mark knew he couldn't take his eyes away from the fight for an instant or be distracted. He spun and thrust with his sword, and Lucilius deflected with his blade. Lucilius made a quick counter and lashed at Mark's throat.

Mark sidestepped, and the blow swished past his face. Lucilius continued the attack, spinning and aiming for Mark's chest.

Mark swung out the Barrett pistol and, with swift aim taken at Lucilius's face, pulled the trigger.

Lucilius reacted quickly and moved his face out of the way, but Mark had anticipated that and compensated. He moved in and stabbed Lucilius in the arm holding the sword.

Lucilius grunted in pain and tried to bridge the gap between them.

Mark aimed and shot Lucilius in the face again — or at least attempted to. Lucilius dodged and retreated this time too, victoriously, but the injury on his arm was still there. He glared at Mark, the injury in his arm healing over.

"You fight without honor. You will die horribly for this!" Lucilius growled as if insulted by the repeated attempts to shoot his face.

"Says the immortal who can't die," Mark scoffed.

He beckoned Lucilius over, and they resumed their deadly dance with a clash of swords.

Gen watched as Mark harried Lucilius. It seemed like a dream. A beautiful and impossible dream. She turned to see her granddad fighting Atticus and the other, Remus.

Spells flew and dissipated as the magic users aimed at each other. Remus produced a bow and arrow and shot at Myrddin.

Gen frowned. There was something off about the arrow. While the whole dream seemed magical with glowing spells and stardust, the tip of the arrow glowed unusually bright in her sight, and she had a sense that she could feel the arrow. The feeling was the same as the nail.

Why was that?

Myrddin moved out of the way of the arrow, and it flew and stuck in the wall. Myrddin became defensive as he had to accommodate for the arrow and defend against Atticus's attacks.

Gen watched as Atticus summoned a large bolt and hurled it at Myrddin. The bolt shot at Myrddin, and Gen felt the air around her warp from its wrongness.

Myrddin braced himself and stopped the bolt inches from his body. His arms were stretched wide as he tried to contain the power of the bolt. He looked to Gen, and she saw the strain on his face as he struggled with Atticus to gain control of the spell.

"Run, Gen," Myrddin shouted.

Gen turned to obey when she saw Remus line up a shot. She turned back and screamed a warning at Myrddin, but her heart knew all too well that it was too late.

The arrow flew out of Remus's bow and headed towards Myrddin. Myrddin saw it coming, but he couldn't release his grip on the bolt Atticus had sent. It was filled with negative energy and would wipe out everything within the containment area. Myrddin knew he could survive, but the same couldn't be said for the others. The lightning bolt had been a feign. The real danger was the arrow.

The arrow flew towards his heart, and within the short span of a moment, Myrddin wondered if he could turn his body away on time or if this was it. It was as if time flew faster than normal, and he couldn't move — not until he saw the arrow reach a couple of inches from his body and wobble to a stop. *Boink!*

What happened?

The arrow strained against a force holding it, and Myrddin's gaze shot up to stare across the room. Gen grunted with the strain of holding the arrow in the air. She had seen the arrow about to pierce her grand-dad's body and did the only thing she could think of. She had called out to the arrow, or rather, the glow on the tip of the arrow. It reminded her of the foot nail.

She had called out, and the arrow had obeyed.

She watched, amazed at herself, confused if what she was thinking was true as the arrow fell to the floor. She looked up to see Remus glowering at her in fear. He nocked another arrow, tightening it, but this time, he aimed at her.

Gen watched the bow in Remus's hand slacken, and the arrow shot forward.

No!

The arrow stopped inches from the sprung bow.

Gen saw Remus back away in fear, and she looked around. She realized what she was doing and what she could be capable of. She could finally help in the fight.

Mark had a shallow cut on his thigh and another under his bicep. Even with his new knowledge, Lucilius was a formidable foe. The slightest break in focus, and he paid for it.

Not that he hadn't held his own.

A cut to Lucilius's forehead gradually healed. His clothes were in shreds from the numerous cuts Mark had placed on him. Any other fight would have been over ages ago, but Lucilius's healing factor made him really immortal.

Mark and Lucilius stalked each other, looking for weaknesses and openings. Like big cats, they knew to observe their prey before pouncing.

131

Mark had learned that Lucilius always feigned to the left before going for a thrust to the heart. He watched as Lucilius balanced on his right heel.

Now!

Lucilius feigned left, and Mark took the bait, moving his sword to intercept the strike. He could feel Lucilius's joy as he struck quickly towards Mark's heart.

Mark had only a couple of bullets left in his pistol but had refrained from using it, making it look like he had run out of ammunition.

The trick wouldn't have worked for someone like him who had spent years with firearms. He subconsciously counted his bullets and those of his teammates. But Lucilius wasn't someone who spent time around guns. He didn't know the intricacies of a gun battle.

Lucilius liked swords.

Mark aimed his pistol at Lucilius's face as he thrust at his heart. Lucilius was surprised as the gun discharged, sending a bullet to his face. Lucilius reacted faster than was humanly possible. He turned his face a fraction out of the way, making the shot that would have pierced his forehead shatter his cheek instead.

He roared in pain, but Mark wasn't through. He spun and swung his sword down, taking Lucilius's arm by the elbow.

Lucilius's bellow turned to a whimper as he fell to his knees.

Mark was winning, but he had no time to lose. He had to make the move now. He didn't hesitate as he went for Lucilius's head, as swift as an arrow.

Gen sent the arrow hurtling towards Atticus. She needed to buy her grand-dad time to deal with the bolt of wrongness. Myrddin had shrunk the bolt into a size smaller than a golf ball, but the bolt pulsated with enough energy that Gen had to look away.

She had a feeling that if her granddad lost his concentration for even a second, they would all perish, and she might have been right.

Atticus saw the bolt coming and waved his hand in a circle. She could see the stress on his face as it scrunched and as his shoulders slumped in fatigue.

It was good to know that they weren't totally invincible.

Atticus must have realized the strength of the arrow coming towards him because he sidestepped the arrow's path, and it brushed his side before piercing into the wall with a thud. It was a very close save, but not quite. Despite his quick move, the arrow did pierce his side.

Atticus grunted in pain as it tore his flesh.

Myrddin finally clenched his palms together, and a flare of light leaked out, and the power of the bolt dissipated. His eyes glowed white as he looked at Atticus and Remus.

Gen felt the build-up of power as Myrddin lashed out at Atticus, sending him bashing through the wall and out of the house.

Mark knew that the fight was over even as he swung his sword victoriously.

His swing was already in motion when he heard a twang and felt the air around him distorted.

Lucilius lay broken on the floor before him, gripping his chopped-off arm in pain. Mark reacted instinctively.

He swung his sword in the direction of the noise and precisely sliced the arrow in two as if air had cut through it. He looked to see Remus back up and aim another arrow. The battle was on.

Mark's hand was a blur as he advanced quickly towards him. Shaft after shaft shattered as he sliced the arrows coming at him into two. Perfect precision of hand. When he approached Remus at a suitable proximity, he swung his sword aiming for Remus's neck. Remus lifted his bow to block, but Mark was already spinning. His first aim was a feign.

Mark's sword sliced through Remus's back, and the man screamed in agony.

Wait…Where was Lucilius?

Gen watched as Myrddin ran after Atticus, and she turned to Mark. Lucilius held his chopped-off hand and seemed to be trying to attach it back to his elbow.

Could they really do that?

Remus was no match for Mark, who swept Remus off his feet with a spinning low kick. He plunged his sword down without hesitating and pinned Remus to the ground. She saw Lucilius stagger to his feet and run out of the living room.

They were beatable.

The accursed now knew fear for the first time in their miserable existence.

Gen's excitement was short-lived, though. It soured when she heard her mother scream.

She rushed out of the house to see her granddad forcing Atticus to his knees. Myrddin didn't touch Atticus, but Atticus struggled with a force that pushed him down onto his knees. Gen saw her granddad's face firm with fury and turned to her mother.

She stood beside her dad, who clutched his shoulder in pain.

No!

Gen rushed to her parents' side, worried. "What happened?"

"One of them fell outside, and your dad tried to be a hero," her mother said. Gen could see that she was worried for her dad, even though she tried to hide it.

"I'm okay, dear. Just got shocked a little."

"Let me see, Dad." Her father shook his head, but Gen was adamant and removed his hand to check his shoulder. Her father's shoulder looked burnt and blistered like he had been poked with a scorching rod.

"You're not okay, Dad. We need to get you to a hospital," she insisted.

"I'll live, Gen. I think we have more pressing matters, don't you think?" Gen bit her lip and looked at the battle raging around her. He was right. They were in the middle of a battlefield, and there were certainly more urgent matters at hand.

Atticus was on his back, a small crater forming around him from the pressure of Myrddin's force. Mark had beaten Remus and Lucilius.

The day seemed over to Gen. At last, they were victorious.

Something that would have been impossible now gleamed with hope, and the accursed were on the defensive for the first time.

Gen felt like leaping for joy. She was free!

She saw Mark step out of the house and smiled. He looked mighty even though he had no weapon on him. Mark saw her, and his face transformed. His eyes lit in… *admiration?* Gen couldn't fathom what feelings Mark had for her, but she knew her heart fluttered when she saw him.

She was about to raise her hand to wave at him when she saw a shadow step behind Mark. Her heart jumped to her throat.

Gen opened her mouth to scream a warning, but it was too late. The tip of a sword burst through Mark's chest, and her world seemed to shatter.

Mark saw Remus struggling weakly against the floor as blood pooled around him. He aimed his pistol at Remus's head when he saw Gen rush out of the room.

He had heard a scream when he had been fighting. Mark looked around the room quickly and noticed that Lucilius was gone.

He hurried after Gen, leaving Remus to his fate. Remus had grown weak from blood loss, and Mark was sure he was out of the fight.

That left Atticus and Lucilius. While he was sure Lucilius was beaten, he wasn't taking any chances.

Gen could be in danger.

He reached the front of the house and saw Gen with her parents.

Gen's mother must have been the source of the scream. She looked all right to Mark, but he noted that Gen's father had a painful grimace on his face.

Myrddin seemed to be winning a contest with Atticus, so Mark sighed in relief as he perceived that there was nothing to be worried about in that direction.

Mark wondered where Lucilius could be hiding. He saw Gen smile at him, and he smiled back.

They had won the fight. Mark had succeeded in keeping her safe.

Mark saw her smile slip as she opened her mouth to scream, and her eyes opened wide. His sense of danger acquired from the memories buried in his soul cried in alarm at him. He tried to move to his left, but pain blossomed in his chest, and his world exploded in pain.

Lucilius felt shame wash over him. He had lived for eons and had never run from a fight. It wasn't him. Lucilius was the oppressor, the one that made his opponents quake in fear. He had borne numerous names over the years — vanquisher of kingdoms, the tyrant in gold, the invisible and indestructible.

For the first time in his life, Lucilius had known fear, and it was a feeling that brought deep hate for the protector in him. Fear...it felt like a knot in his heart.

He had vanquished the protector's ancestors, hunted them for pleasure or sport.

Now he felt what it was like to be the hunted.

His cut-off arm still hurt even though the bones and muscles had knitted back together. It felt sore and tender to the touch. He would be useless with that arm and hand for months as the nerves repaired themselves and mobility came back, and the thought scared him. He held his sword in his left hand, though the feeling was foreign and uncomfortable.

Remus had saved his life. Lucilius wasn't sure any of them could survive with their heads cut off.

They could be killed. Marius had shown them that.

That blasted bearer of the nails had burnt Marius out of existence. The bearer was a thing to be feared, which was why they had hunted their lineage down. They had thought they had gotten the last of them when Myrddin had vanished from the face of the earth.

Lucilius had taken pleasure in killing the little girl in France.

Over the years, he had honed his skill with the sword to make him unbeatable.

That had amounted to nothing in the face of things.

Beaten by a whelp, a babe in the ocean of time.

He could not allow that to happen.

Lucilius had thought of escaping into the night but had turned back to the house. He had seen the fight between Myrddin and Atticus but had ignored them. Sneaking into the house, he got to the living room to see Remus pinned to the wooden floor with his sword.

Mark was standing at the front of the house, looking like the conqueror of nations. And it stirred Lucilius's fear and anger. He still had one last trick he rarely showed. There had been no need, as he hadn't faced a foe worthy of pushing him to this extreme, but it appeared that now it was needed.

Atticus had magic. Remus could disguise his appearance and become anyone he wished. Marius had had the power in his word. They were all difficult to kill, as they eventually healed from all wounds, he being the quickest to do that.

Their enemies had thought that the healing factor was his ability, but they were wrong.

He stood out amongst his peers in one area — he could cancel any trace of his existence. He could be beside a prey, and even magic wouldn't detect him.

Lucilius exercised that ability as he moved silently towards Mark, eyeing him carefully as his prey. He got behind Mark and was close enough to touch him when he saw Gen looking at him. The victorious look on the girl's face turned into fear, and the taste of it made Lucilius feel powerful again.

Within a few seconds, before Mark could turn, Lucilius smiled wickedly as he plunged his sword into Mark's back.

Gen's cry was a lament that pierced the night and shattered the containment barrier around them. Myrddin blasted Atticus further into the ground and raced to Gen's side.

She was on her knees with her hands stretched out towards the house, tears burning her eyes and cheeks and stinging them red.

Myrddin looked at the front of the house and saw a shadow dart inside.

Mark lay on his knees with a sword thrust through his chest, and his pistol clattered to the ground. As Mark tipped to the side, Myrddin caught him with a gentle gust of wind. He pulled Mark towards them and gently rested him on the porch, careful not to let him bleed further. Mark's face was ashen, and Myrddin couldn't detect any heartbeat. This wasn't good.

"Save him!" Gen cried out to Myrddin, but he only shook his head.

If there had been something to hold on to, a faint heartbeat, maybe Myrddin could have been able to latch onto that, but there was nothing.

Gen groaned in anguish as she rushed over to Mark and cradled his head.

"Take us to the hospital, Myrddin."

"Honey, I don't think—" Gen's mother started.

"Please." Gen looked at Myrddin with tears in her eyes. The look cut into Myrddin's soul, and he didn't have the heart to tell her that Mark was gone. Myrddin nodded and swirled his hand above them, gathering his power.

As the sky appeared a greyer shade, they vanished in the air.

CHAPTER NINETEEN

Myrddin and the others materialized in St. Philip's Memorial Hospital in the blink of an eye.

Myrddin staggered and leaned against a pillar, breathing heavily.

Translocation or teleportation, as it was commonly known, wasn't an easy feat. It tasked the spirit and soul heavily, and Myrddin only did it when it was absolutely needed, and never twice in one day. It consumed all his energy.

Not only had he done it more than three times in the last twenty-four hours, but he had also carried more people than he had in centuries.

His spirit seemed to contract within itself as it suffered from over-burning. To the natural eye, it would seem as though he had had a heart attack as suddenly, he couldn't breathe, and a sharp pain pierced his heart.

Myrddin clutched his chest and slumped to the floor. Gen watched in fear and confusion, unable to think about what was to be done.

Their arrival had created a stir as people panicked and screamed.

"Help! Please, I need help!" Gen shouted, looking around, begging everyone to do something.

Her cry motivated some brave souls to come to their aid, and Myrddin almost passed out in relief.

A gurney was wheeled in, and Mark was placed on it. A doctor approached Myrddin, but he waved the woman away. There was nothing orthodox medicine could do for him. He was going to be okay, he hoped. He only needed rest. His spirit would naturally heal if given enough time.

Myrddin watched as Gen followed the doctors surrounding Mark. Gen's parents walked to Myrddin and sat on the floor beside him.

"It doesn't look good, does it, Myrddin?" Mr. Isherwood asked.

Myrddin shook his head. He could barely say a word as he gripped his heart tightly. His face scrunched in pain. It wasn't passing anytime soon from the intensity that he felt.

"You okay, Dad?" Mrs. Isherwood asked, concern in her voice.

Myrddin nodded.

"Spell overuse," Myrddin croaked. It was the simplest explanation he could give at the moment.

"Can we help?" she asked. Myrddin shook his head, wishing that everyone would stop asking him questions.

"Does it hurt?" Gen's dad said, and Martha hit his shoulder. Gen's dad grunted in pain.

"Will he make it? I've never seen Genesis so distraught," Martha asked.

"Don't know." Myrddin hoped there was something medical science could do. He had seen the sword pierce Mark's heart. To be honest, he did not feel hopeful.

Unlike the last time, Mark had been alive when he had arrived. He had been able to cast a healing spell, and the magic had anchored to Mark's soul.

Myrddin hadn't sensed Mark's soul this time around. His healing spell would have dissipated with nothing to hold on to.

Gen felt something break within her. She thought hearing about her grand-dad's death was the worst thing that could ever happen to her.

She had been wrong.

Her heart felt broken. She walked woodenly along the aisle and stopped when a doctor told her she couldn't go beyond that spot. Gen heard herself mutter something to the doctor, but she couldn't connect to the here and now. She seemed disassociated with the events unfolding before her.

Mark can't die. He can't!

In such a short time, he had come to mean so much to her. A pillar she could lean on, someone she could depend on. And she felt worse because she never had the chance to tell him how she felt and how important he was to her.

Gen wiped her cheeks and realized she had been crying.

When did that happen?

Her world was lost. She could not focus on anything for now and stood in the center of the aisle as people walked around her. No one tried to move her out of the way or console her.

An orderly passed her with a bucket and mop. The strong smell of bleach and hospital disinfectant assaulted her nose.

She stood, and she waited. For a miracle, maybe.

A doctor came out of the operating room, and one look on his face told her all she needed to know.

No!

Gen shook her head.

He couldn't go yet. Mark was her protector. That's what her granddad had called him. He couldn't leave her unprotected.

Gen felt a hand on her arm and looked up to see a doctor talking to her.

"I'm so sorry. The injury was severe and had punctured one of the ventricles of the heart. There was nothing we could do."

Her soul shattered into a million little pieces. She could not believe it, but she realized that this was reality and that she needed to see him before she couldn't anymore.

"I want to see him," she pleaded with a defeated look in her eyes.

"I'm sorry, but you—"

"Please. I need to see him." She begged, holding back from screaming as it took all her strength to even stand there.

The doctor sighed and nodded. He led her to the theater and opened the door.

With her heart beating faster than ever, Gen walked in slowly and felt the door swing shut behind her.

❖

Atticus climbed out of the crater and slumped face-first on the ground. He was exhausted, and his clothes were shredded from the blast of Myrddin's scorching wind.

How could the wind be so hot? His skin felt scorched and red, and only his shield had saved him from Myrddin's power. He saw a shadow and looked up. Remus walked out of the Isherwood house, looking as terrible as Atticus felt.

"What happened to you?" he asked as he sat up.

Remus grimaced in anger.

"The day has gone unexpectedly."

"That would be an understatement. I never thought I'd see the day when we would retreat in defeat," Remus grunted.

"And where is our mighty leader?"

Atticus saw another figure walk out of the house. Lucilius looked terrible. Worse than either of them. One of his arms hung uselessly by his side. His clothes were slightly better than Atticus's, but his face looked like he had just seen a ghost.

"I take it things didn't go well with you, too." Atticus tried not to smile.

He never said that he was better than Myrddin, but Lucilius acted like the world's best warrior, and apparently, he had been challenged well.

He looked highly shaken now. Did the girl's protector really do this to Lucilius?

"What do we do now?" Remus asked.

"I sense the nail is close," Atticus said.

"I say we regroup and strategize," Lucilius suggested.

"I still say that we get what we came for. You took out the protector. The guardian is weak right now. That will make it three against one." Lucilius glared at Atticus, but he refused to back down. Lucilius didn't look so high and mighty now. After all, he had tasted a human trait — fear. He had trembled, and it made him realize just how wrong he was about himself.

Maybe he could take him down and become the leader of the group.

"You don't know the state Myrddin's in. That will be a risk we can't afford."

"Everything is a risk, Lucilius. We have been chasing this nail for so long I've forgotten when we started. We have the chance to end this."

"We still don't have the third nail," Remus pointed out, but Atticus waved his observation aside.

"Getting the last nail is easy. We know where it is, and we won't have this opposition. I say now is the best time to grab this nail."

"Okay, but you go alone," Lucilius conceded, and Atticus smiled.

"I'll need Remus's help." Lucilius had already turned and walked away, and Atticus gritted his teeth.

"Are you sure about this?"

"Come on, let's go!"

Atticus felt good about his chances. They had lost tonight, but the fight wasn't over. They could make a comeback.

Myrddin must be weak now, he told himself.

Atticus had felt Myrddin teleport out of the area, and he knew what it took to move one body to a new location.

Myrddin must be weak right now.

Remus shook his head. "I think I'll sit this one out, my friend. My gut tells me only more trouble will come out of this."

Atticus fumed. He knew Remus was cowardly sometimes, but couldn't they see the opportunity here?

"This is our chance to turn things around."

"Don't be upset, Atticus. It's just that since we started pursuing the bearer and this nail, there have been unexpected turns of events. Who knew Lucilius could be hurt this bad? And Myrddin appearing? We have always made it a rule to avoid his involvement."

"You may have Remus, but even the great Myrddin has his limits. And I can assure you; he has reached his."

"You don't need me for this one, then. Your invisibility spell will take you anywhere. Just be careful. This has been all unexpected." Remus clapped Atticus's shoulder for a moment and walked away.

Atticus took a deep breath and focused. He missed Marius. He had been a joy to work with, and he could sweet-talk anyone into doing his will. Marius would have jumped at the opportunity to end this.

Blast that nail bearer. The woman had been the cause of Marius's death.

Atticus had always admired Marius's powers. He even tried to find the spell to allow him to have Marius's ability, but it had proved impossible. Determined, he could sense the nail miles ahead of him and began walking in that direction, unnerved about whether the accursed accompany him or not.

It ends tonight.

❖

Gen stared at the body on the operating table. She walked closer and stood by the table. His body had been covered with a surgical drape, leaving his face exposed. There was a square cut on the drape around his chest region where the doctors had worked.

He looks so peaceful, Gen thought as tears rolled down her cheeks. She reached out gently and brushed a strand of hair from his face.

"Please don't leave me," she whispered. She wasn't sure she could survive the pain of losing Mark.

Gen's hand hovered over Mark's body, and she felt the pulsating power of the nail in his pocket. With hands trembling and with a wavering hope that some good may come, she pulled out the handkerchief and spread it open on Mark's body.

With grim determination, she grabbed the nail and, as she had presumed, was transported away.

❖

She was back at Golgotha.

Gen looked up at the cross of Calvary, where the Nazarene was hung between two thieves. Gen heard Him groan in pain and shuddered.

Jesus was still alive.

She looked at the multitude that had gathered at the base of the small hill. A few lamented and wept while most flung insults and jeered at

Jesus. It hurt Gen, and she couldn't help but wonder how it was a bizarre place to be at.

Indignation welled up in Gen, and she took a step forward.

He is suffering for you, idiots; she wanted to yell at them.

"You healed others and raised the dead. Save yourself now," someone yelled in spite.

"He says he is the Christ. Let him come down from there, and I will believe." There was a chorus of laughter from the men around the speaker.

Jesus groaned in pain again.

"Father, forgive them, for they are ignorant of their actions." The words were a whisper, said from dying lips, but they thundered in Gen's heart and resonated in her soul. She felt shame flood her heart at the thoughts that anger at the crowd had produced. *How could they do this to Him?*

The crowd still laughed and jested.

"I thirst," Jesus said.

Someone took a cloth and dampened it in a liquid. The person lifted the fabric and offered it up to Jesus, who took a sip. Jesus turned away from the vinegar-soaked cloth, and the man laughed.

The defilement continued, and Gen found herself on her knees in tears. She could not see how humans could behave like such monsters. Did they have no hearts?

Why? Why make Him suffer so much?

Words flooded her soul, first as a whisper and louder but gentle at the same time.

"I have come. That man may have abundant life."

"Truly, I say this to you, except a corn of wheat falls to the ground and dies. It abides alone. But if it dies, it brings forth much fruit."

"I am the resurrection and the life. Anyone that believes in me and is dead shall surely live again."

"For I have come to save that which is lost."

The words continued and rose to a crescendo in Gen's heart. Gen looked and saw that her heart had begun to glow, and the light emerging from her chest was getting brighter and brighter.

What was happening?

Atticus had woven an invisibility spell around himself. He could feel the nail close by, and he did not want to lose it.

The pull from the nail had led him to a hospital, and Atticus had been momentarily surprised when he had seen Myrddin sitting close to the emergency door. The young bearer's parents sat with Myrddin, but Atticus couldn't see the bearer anywhere.

Atticus shied away from Myrddin and crept to the door. He waited by the door until someone came close, and the door slid open. He couldn't afford to make his presence felt and dimmed his power as he followed the visitor into the hospital.

Atticus's skin tingled in anticipation. The nail was so close.

He could feel it radiating from a room close by. He would have to make a decisive strike before Myrddin could intervene. Atticus gathered as much of his power as he could and walked towards the door that called to him.

Myrddin wondered when Gen would come out.

He hadn't wanted to be the bearer of bad news, but he felt the doctors should have told her the truth.

He would have to be there for her during this period of her grief.

Myrddin remembered Empress Helena and her sorrow when her grandson, Crispus, had been executed. He had been reluctant to tell her that it had been the work of the enemy, who had sensed the Almighty's hand on her life.

She had overcome that grief, and her end had been better than her beginning. This was all anyone could ask for.

Myrddin sensed a flicker of power and frowned. He looked around the hospital and focused inward. He was suffering from spiritual overburn, but he could still reach out to the spiritual realm and see if everything was okay. That was the least he could do.

Myrddin spread his senses out and didn't notice anything out of the ordinary. Maybe it was time to meet up with Gen.

Myrddin struggled to his feet.

"Where are you going, Dad?" Martha asked.

"I don't think it's wise to leave Gen alone."

"Give her a little time. She needs closure," Mr. Isherwood suggested.

Myrddin grunted but continued walking to the hospital door. One thing this night had taught him was to be prepared for the unexpected.

He wouldn't put it past those cursed brutes to try and take advantage of their weakness. He was close to the door when there was an explosion of light. A blinding beam blasted, and he was blown backward.

CHAPTER TWENTY

Gen opened her eyes, and she was back in the operating theater. The sound of hospital activities seemed extremely loud in her ears.

Gen saw that she was glowing. The light had consumed her whole body. She still had a hold on the nail, and she looked at Mark's body lying on the theater table.

Jesus had said that He was the resurrection and the life.

The resurrection and the life. It struck her.

Gen placed her hand on Mark's body and spoke with conviction. "Let him live!"

She wasn't sure that it would work, but she watched in anticipation. His body remained still on the table. Gen wasn't shaken by what she was seeing. Instead, she looked inwards and saw that she was thrumming with power.

Her vision had proven one thing to her — Jesus had been moved with love for humanity and was willing to give His life for it.

She remembered a saying her granddad had whispered to her many years ago as he tucked her in for the night.

No greater love than this; that a man should die for a friend.

Love was the power, she realized.

She allowed her feelings for Mark to well up to the surface, and the power thrummed louder. She looked down at Mark's body as the theater door opened before she could tell him what she felt. A blackness swelled around the door.

The accursed. They had come.

Anger filled her soul. Anger that they would try and interrupt the moment and snatch the tiny window of opportunity. She felt she had to bring Mark back by any means now. She wasn't angry that they had come for the nails. She was mad that they would try and hurt Mark again.

She saw flickering red lightning shoot out of the darkness and hurl towards her.

Static filled the room, igniting little pieces of surgical cloth and material. Gen did not run.

She would protect Mark's body, even if it cost her life, just like he did for her.

❖

Atticus had seen the light spill out of the room ahead of him and created a shield in time as it exploded in power and washed around him.

He felt the edges of his clothes smoke as the light burned around him. It felt burning hot.

Quickly he ran to the room and pushed open the door.

Myrddin would definitely sense that and come running. He couldn't afford that.

Atticus saw the bearer standing over the dead protector and flung all the power he had gathered at her.

There would be no saving this one tonight.

The nail was finally his.

❖

Myrddin staggered to his feet. The spiritual fatigue was gone. He knew he was needed at this very moment.

His soul and spirit felt refreshed and whole.

He didn't spend time puzzling over what had happened but rushed into the hospital.

He saw the reception area in disarray. People were slumped on the floor while some looked at him in a dazed and confused manner. Myrddin saw a theater door open and felt the discharge of powerful dark magic.

Atticus!

Myrddin felt a weight in his heart as he ran to the room. No one could survive that blast. He felt defeated for a moment.

❖

Gen staggered back a step as the lightning bolt slammed into her. She looked at her body as it rippled with electricity, and her fingers released sparks.

She felt…normal. While nothing was normal around her at the time, she felt stronger than ever.

Atticus had dismissed his invisibility spell, giving him the chance to conjure the lightning bolt, and he lay spent on his feet. His eyes opened in amazement as he saw Gen still standing on her feet, looking practically unhurt.

Another whisper filled her heart, and she turned to stare at Atticus.

And the light shines in the darkness, and the darkness cannot comprehend or understand it.

Atticus fell back against the door. She blazed with so much light that his clothes smarted smoking. White fire spilled out of her eyes as she stared at him in anger. Atticus was confused. *What was happening?*

He had to escape, for he saw his doom as sure as day, and he had to do it now!

Gen placed her hand on Mark's chest and turned again to Atticus. Summoning all the power she felt inside her, she allowed it to burst forth, and she spoke gently, "Live again."

Light spilled out of her, pouring out of every opening it could find. It filled the room and washed out.

Atticus got to the door and opened it when the white fire caught up to him.

He felt unimaginable pain as the light consumed every darkness in him. It burnt him alive.

His deeds flashed before his eyes. The lives he had taken, the innocents and infants he had sacrificed over the years for power. For the first time, he felt disgusted with himself. He saw the monster that he was.

He eventually saw himself at the foot of the cross at Golgotha, laughing and jeering, spitting at the foot of the Christ hung on the cross between two criminals.

Atticus screamed in pain and continued to cry out as he was consumed. He felt each part of his body shatter, shredding into particles and drifting into the air until he felt empty...non-existent.

Laughter.

Mocking laughter echoed all around Mark.

He looked around, and all he saw was a white haze.

Mark recognized that voice. A twist between a sneer and a grin. Mark had hated that sound. Hated it and the person that made it.

Billy Bones.

The terror of the third grade.

The white mist evaporated, and Mark saw that he was back home. He remembered dying.

The piercing pain through his heart had vibrated through his soul. He knew he was dead, but he had expected something…different.

Definitely not Billy Bones.

He remembered that day. A part of his life imprinted in his memories. *How do you forget your worst day?*

Mark felt pulled to the scene unfolding before him.

It was a playground, and a ring of children chanted around two children. Well, three, if you counted Little Joe Macpherson.

Little Joe lay curled up on the ground as he tried to avoid Billy Bones's punches.

One of his classmates told Little Joe to stand up for himself, and Little Joe had refused to give his lunch to Billy.

Billy had not taken it in his stride as the classmate had thought.

That classmate had been him.

A younger version of Mark stood over Little Joe and glared at Billy Bones. Younger Mark had a split lip and a shiner, but that didn't reduce the intensity of the glare younger Mark shot at Billy Bones.

The crowd of chanting children expected a fight, but young Mark hadn't given it to them that day or any other day.

That had emboldened Billy, and young Mark had endured a period of torment as Billy Bones included him on his *beat-em-up* list.

"What's going on here?" a voice asked, and the ring of children scattered like dry leaves blown by a gentle breeze.

Mark frowned as he saw a man walk to his younger version. Like all bullies, Billy Bones had done a disappearing act worthy of the great Houdini.

Mark vaguely recollected being saved by a stranger that day. The man looked down at Mark and smiled.

"It's hard standing for what's right, isn't it, Marcus?"

Young Mark looked at the man with suspicion. How had he known his full name?

He had been given the name Marcus Reynolds, but everybody called him Mark.

"Especially when you know you could have beaten that bully."

That was what had made everything worse for Mark. He knew he could have hurt Billy Bones badly, and he chose not to.

His father had been in the army and had taught Mark self-defense from an early age. Mark could have struck at Billy Bones in a thousand ways and really hurt him, but something inside him had made him stay his hand.

But how had the stranger known?

"Don't worry, Marcus, you have a great destiny to fulfill."

The stranger looked up from the younger Mark and stared directly at Mark.

"Welcome, Marcus."

Mark gazed into the friendly face of the stranger.

"Who are you? Mark asked, but he knew.

There was no mistaking the feeling of love, peace, and acceptance he felt in the presence of the stranger. He wasn't really a stranger.

"Is this memory real? All of it?"

"Yes, it is. Do you remember how you felt afterward?"

Mark thought back to that day years ago.

He had gone home feeling...happy. He remembered he had been humming to a beat as he walked home, split lip and all.

"It was you then, wasn't it?"

The man smiled in his divine glow.

"So, I'm dead then," Mark said, remembering the pain from being pierced by a sword.

"Yes, your body lies on the theater table. Genesis has bought you these few minutes we have presently."

Mark sighed.

In the end, he had failed her. *Would she be all right?*

"Don't worry about the nail bearer, Marcus. She still has a lot to do."

"So, this is the end of the line for me, then?"

"That depends, Marcus," the man said, giving Mark a ray of hope.

"On what?" Mark's curiosity was piqued. Could there be a chance to go back?

"You have fought a good fight, Marcus Reynolds. You can come home."

"But?"

"There is still more to do. The enemy grows bolder every day, and the evil that seeks to devour the nail bearer grows bolder. She will need all the help she can get."

Mark smiled. He wanted to be back with her. He wanted to protect her and stand by her side. Always.

"What are we waiting for?"

The man smiled at Mark, and the world went white.

Gen was in a vision, and she knew it.

She was in a wheat field. The air smelt clean and fresh around her, and the sun was warm on her cheeks. There was a moment of contentment, but that was quickly shattered as the world turned dark around her. A thick cloud of darkness took over the field.

She felt the ground below her feet tremble before a beast broke from the ground and rose before her. Gigantic and enormous, it loomed over her. Genesis saw the beast shrouded in the darkest blackness she could have imagined.

The beast roared and swept its hand across the wheat field in what seemed to be an angry movement.

A quarter of the wheat burnt and blackened as the beast's hand swept over them, with slight embers fading off from them.

No.

Gen did not feel scared but felt anger at the beast's action. The beast raised its hand to make another swipe, and Gen raced forward.

She stretched out her hand in a stopping motion and felt a light burst out of her. The light ate at the darkness, and the beast recoiled. It roared its anger at Gen and looked down at her with eyes like pits of burning fire.

Gen knew she had to protect the field from the beast. She naturally felt like it was her duty.

The beast swung down, and Gen braced herself. She felt its darkness slam into her light, and she dropped to a knee.

Whispers filled the air around her. Doubt and despair scratched at the edges of her light.

She could feel the pressure bearing down on her, and the weight of the darkness sought to crush her.

You are nothing, the whispers crooned, but Gen knew the lie for what it was.

She had the light within her, and she believed in it. It was her belief that had kept her going, and she would not listen to any evil whispers now.

Gen felt a presence walk up to her and saw her grandad stand beside her. He cupped his hands together and gradually separated them, revealing a swirling glow of bright light. The light burst from his hands and struck the beast down.

Gen watched as people came from out of the wheat field and stood beside her.

There was a young teenage girl with a blue bangle on her wrist.

A man in his mid-forties stood by her granddad's side.

A schoolteacher wearing a plain blouse and a pleated skirt hurried over and joined the group.

A doctor, wearing his scrubs and surgical gloves, stepped out.

They all stretched out their hands and released light at the colossal beast, all forming one huge beam of light.

Gen looked around in bewilderment. Apart from her granddad, the others were strangers to her.

The seven shall prevail.

It was a whisper that grew louder with every passing second.

Victory comes through the hands of the seven.

Who are the seven? Gen wondered as she looked around her. A quick headcount showed that there were five people with her.

That made six, including her. Why did the voice keep saying seven?

Gen felt a hand gently rest on her shoulder. The touch carried warmth and such a depth of emotion that Gen didn't need to turn around to know who the hand belonged to. Her ears became warm from nervousness.

Her heart suddenly felt complete and more power than she had ever felt coursed through her and slammed into the beast.

The beast reeled back, hurt and afraid. It staggered to balance itself and looked at the people around Gen with hate-filled eyes before locking eyes with Gen.

The darkness around the beast suddenly pulled inwards, and to Gen's joy, the beast stumbled and disappeared into a portal that opened and immediately closed.

Gen turned around to see Mark smiling at her. She hugged him tightly as tears ran down her face.

"Tell me this is real," she whispered to herself.

Let it be real.

Gen felt hands pat her shoulders in reassurance, and she tried to memorize the faces of the people standing around her.

It seemed very important that she knew who the strangers were.

She would need all the help she could get in the coming battle with the red dragon.

Mark opened his eyes to see the harsh glare of the fluorescent tubes on the ceiling. He felt a weight on his stomach and looked down to see Gen resting on him.

"Gen," he said, his throat feeling parched. His head hammered painfully as he tried to get a bearing.

He remembered fighting Lucilius…and winning.

The last thing he remembered was waving at Gen and then feeling a pain, unlike anything he had ever felt before.

Had he died?

He had had the strangest dream.

Had that been real?

He remembered the incident, but only vaguely. And if the dream was true, then that meant he had an encounter with...Jesus...as a kid?

Had He been involved in his life ever since?

Mark looked around and saw that he was in an operating theater, which meant he was in a hospital.

The door swung open, and Myrddin walked in. He looked at Mark and stumbled in surprise, amazed at seeing him alive. His expression confirmed Mark's fear that something terrible must have happened to him.

He must have *died*.

"Mark?"

Mark tried to reply, but his voice came out in a squeaky form, so he nodded. Myrddin looked relieved until he turned to Gen and saw that she wasn't responding.

Myrddin shook Gen gently, but she didn't respond. He whispered some words that were too faint for Mark to hear or comprehend, and Gen gasped.

Mark looked at Myrddin in surprise.

He had seen Myrddin's hand glow white briefly as he chanted. A thin white thread of magic had gone from Myrddin's hand and entered Gen.

What the...he could see magic?

That couldn't be possible, but there it was. Myrddin's hand continued to glow, and Mark saw Gen take a deep breath.

"It's good to have you back," Myrddin said.

"Wha...what...are you do...doing to...her?"

"Checking to see if she's okay."

"What's wr...wrong?"

"Nothing. Gen's probably exhausted. A lot of spiritual power was released here, and seeing you up and about, I have a feeling she had a hand in that."

Mark looked back at Gen.

Had she brought him back? Was that even possible?

Myrddin shook Gen gently by the shoulder, and she stirred. She opened her eyes and looked at Mark.

"Welcome back, Gen. How are you feeling?" Myrddin asked.

"I...I can't see," she stuttered.

Mark noticed the difference in her eyes. He had been too exhausted to see it before, but as Gen looked around in fear and confusion, Mark saw that her eyes had gone completely white.

N

EPILOGUE

Josephine Jones hated her name. Her mother had loved the story of Napoleon Bonaparte and his first wife, Josephine. Josephine's childhood had been one of jests and taunts, but she had taken it in her stride.

She had left Saskatchewan as a teenager and had vowed never to return, but here she was, years later, in the same town she thought was in her past.

Josephine tried to ignore the throbbing pain in her back. She was tired of feeling it.

She knew she was dying, and there was nothing anybody could do about it.

The doctors had said the growth had not been detected early and had become incurable. The pain in her back had grown until she was now utterly bedridden in St. Philip's Memorial Hospital.

It would be any moment now. The cancerous growth had spread to most of the nerves surrounding the pancreas. Painkillers were Josephine's staple diet, but even these could not dull the pain anymore.

Josephine heard a commotion outside her door as a body hit against it and slumped. She turned her head and grimaced because the movement cost her. Pain blossomed inside her, and she almost passed out.

Josephine stared in amazement as a bright light seemed to radiate from the door and sweep across the room. She felt warmth wrap around her as the light engulfed her.

Josephine saw the light fill her vision and everything in the hospital room.

She turned and noticed she was on her feet.

What was going on?

The pain was gone. She took a deep breath and laughed in relief.

Was she dreaming?

As the light pulsed away, she realized that she was staring at her hand.

She wasn't feeling any pain. She stood in the center of the room in wonder.

She was healed. *Wasn't she?*

153

The vital signs monitor's synchronous beep interrupted the monotonous feel Theo had as he watched his father lying on the hospital bed. He felt numb as the respirator kept his dad alive.

The doctor's prognosis wasn't good, and he had said Liam wouldn't make it through the night.

Theo heard the commotion by the hospital room door and frowned. He got up slowly from his seat and walked towards the door when he felt a light wash over him.

Theo staggered, his childhood flashing rapidly before his eyes.

The sensation was instantly over, leaving Theo confused.

He looked around the room and fell back in surprise when he saw his father sitting upright on the bed.

Liam looked around in bewilderment and noticed Theo.

"Theo?"

"Dad? Oh my God!"

Theo rushed to his dad's bedside and hugged his father.

"I'm so glad you're okay."

Theo released his dad, and Liam looked around in confusion.

"I saw it, son. I saw it."

"Saw what, Dad?"

Liam turned and looked Theo in the eyes.

"I saw the pearly gates."

Lucilius sat and tried not to fidget. The waiting room was beautifully furnished with a Persian rug at the center of the room. He had his fingers crossed.

Remus sat beside him, and Lucilius saw his knee twitch nervously.

They had a right to be nervous, but Lucilius would show no fear, even when he felt it.

He was immortal and couldn't be killed. He would bear all that would be placed on him.

A soft tapping sound filtered into Lucilius's ears, and he turned to see a pretty young woman walk into the room.

"He will see you now," she said and turned to lead the way as her heels tapped on the wooden floor.

Lucilius gritted his teeth as he got to his feet and followed the woman.

"Do you think he is in a good mood?" Remus asked as he followed Lucilius.

Lucilius ignored Remus's question. He would not be infected with the cowardice that seemed to ooze from Remus's pores. He would see his end standing with his head held high.

They walked past a fountain with a mermaid statue and moved to another section of the house.

The young woman stopped before a door and knocked once. She opened the door and gestured Lucilius and Remus in. Lucilius walked past the woman and entered what looked like a room meant for hosting dignitaries.

The chandelier gave off a weird blue light that made the room look strange and seemed to suck the little confidence Lucilius was holding on to.

The man they had come to see was sitting on a posh leather settee. He had a glass of wine which he stirred with a finger as he waited for Lucilius and Remus to stand before him.

There was nothing ominous about the man. He looked middle-aged with a slender body that fitted the designer suit he was dressed in.

The man didn't offer them a seat, so Lucilius and Remus were forced to remain standing. They towered over the man, but Lucilius could feel the fear coming off Remus. He may be a coward, but he had justifiable reasons to fear the man sitting before them.

"It really was a simple job." The man was soft-spoken and calm. He continued to stir his wine.

"Myrddin was there."

The words stopped the man's hand, and he looked up. He had a handsome face that most women would find appealing, but his eyes told a different story. Maybe others wouldn't notice, but Lucilius saw it. He looked like he was from hell.

The man sitting before them was ancient. The eyes told stories of times and seasons that had passed and gone before it.

"We calculated for his interference, didn't we?" the man said. Remus had the good sense to keep quiet and look at the floor. The man turned to Lucilius.

"What do you have to say for yourself?"

"There were unforeseen circumstances. The nail bearer grew into her powers faster than we thought."

"One girl. You lot couldn't defeat a simple scared girl. This was the right time to destroy the nails, and you couldn't deliver."

"Myrddin—"

"You came to me cursed. Cursed and broken, and I gave you purpose."

"All isn't lost. If you give me more men, I can…"

The man raised a finger, and Lucilius felt a vice clamp over him. A pressure pressed against him and rattled his insides. It took all his strength to remain standing.

He would die on his feet if he had to.

Suddenly the pressure left him, and he gasped.

"It is not your purview to concern yourselves with the nails. You will hand over the nail in your possession."

Lucilius was taken aback. He had chased the nails for as long as he could remember. To just hand it over wasn't something he had thought about.

"I know we failed now, but we can—"

"I will assign Asmodeus to the task of getting the nail."

"Asmodeus will destroy everything he touches. He will destroy the nails."

"That's perfectly acceptable."

"But we need the nails. We will remain vagabonds for eternity."

"A befitting punishment, don't you think?" It wasn't a question. Lucilius felt anger well up within him.

Maybe it was time to strike out on his own.

Follow Gen's journey, as her powers
continue to manifest in ways astonishing to behold!

But even with the support of her new-found allies, will her
strength be great enough to defeat the most powerful of the Accursed,
a creature hell-bent on possession of the nails of power?

Find out in FOOTNAIL Book 2: Forging the Sword!

FOOTNAIL

BOOK 2: FORGING THE SWORD

Akorede Adekoya &
Howard Haugom